CHIZURU
1945

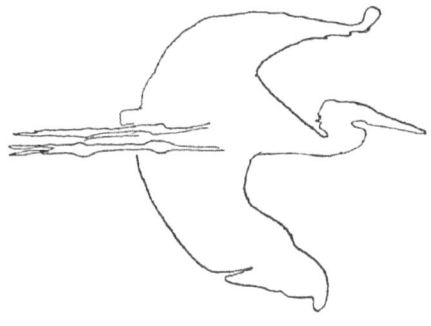

Donald J. Mangus

Chizuru 1945 is dedicated to
Sadako S., Akemi, Terumi, the Kandas
and all the children.

Prologue

Much of this story is true. It started with a deadly conflagration many years ago. Some of the people are real, though the names have been turned around. References to Charles E. Ives and Bela Bartòk are unreservedly meant to represent real data and facts.

Many of the personae may have walked with us, or may be ghosts from a thousand dreams of yours and mine. Whether they ever existed, or will exist, is a question I cannot answer, but rather leave it to the reader to decide.

In Central Park, New York, in the winter of 1938, Eben Adams met a young Jennifer—a strangely isolated and evanescent child. Their story is timeless and illusory. "I know a song, "Jennie says. "Would you like to hear it?" — and thus:

> "Where I come from
> Nobody knows;
> And where I'm going
> Everything goes.

The wind blows,
The sea flows —
And nobody knows."

Jennie's haunting song from "A Portrait of Jennie" seems tuneless and rootless. A paean from an apparition perhaps? Yet Robert Nathan no doubt was aware of Thoreau's early poem, "Men Say They Know Many Things." To extrapolate:

Men say they know
many things;
But lo' they have
taken wings –
....
The wind that blows
Is all that anybody knows.

Too similar for coincidence, but why not? The impression and influence of one creative mind on another is as acceptable and predictable as the genetic pressure a specific twist of DNA exerts on the son and the daughter, who become at once the summation of the parent genes, and the transcendent multiple of the best and the worst of those biological directives.

In 1958, a nurse by the name of Loretta Se-galla presented me with my first copy of Paul Gallico's "The Snow Goose." I have never been without that book since then. I have read and reread that minimalist masterpiece over and over again.

Almost thirty years later, in 1987, I came upon Robert Nathan's "Portrait of Jennie," published approximately the same time as "The Snow Goose." The book was given to me by the real "Akemi."

During those intervening years and recalling childhood days during the turbulent years of World War II, when the "world was on fire," I experienced firsthand some of the magic found in each work. It is a combination of actual people and events, and those two timeless stories, that inspired "Chizuru."

If the writing of this story does anything, it expresses the parallel reflections of three authors, two professional and one a hopeless amateur, on the subtle and sometimes inexplicable happenings of passing souls (some actual and fixed in time, and some perhaps not), and of the goodness to be discovered in them.

Can there be, was there ever a Fritha or a Phillip? Did Eben and Jennie ever walk hand in hand in Central Park? And what of Sadako and Akemi and Terumi?

Is it possible that these ephemeral protagonists were tangible and real, or merely ghostly phantoms of the imagination, casting no shadows?

I suggest that there is more substance here than not, and that the shadows are real.

It is said that although the old are wise, it is the young who will open the doors to Creation. It is also said that the Child cannot be wasted, but will be sent instead to give life to the barren, joy to the mourning, and love to the forgotten.

CHIZURU

1945

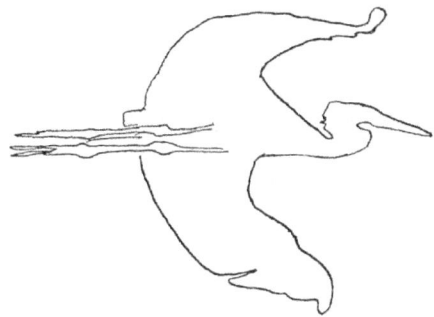

Chapter I

The great Firestorm ended the lives of so many of the children — long before their time.

But Fate predestined otherwise, and Providence could not allow such waste. Thus, their spirits were sent afar, to seek out purpose and need. And not until each soul they touched was positively transformed could the children return again to gaze upon their Destiny.

There is a kind of cold that penetrates more deeply than others.

On that evening in Chicago in 1944, as I stepped from the warm halls of the University Performing Arts Center, that cold, carried on a stinging January wind, struck my face. I reflexly sucked in my breath and pulled my scarf tighter across my neck and chest.

The crowd was leaving the concert hall quietly, the gentle murmur of approbation for a performance well done filling the icy air. I remember the old pleasure of rubber boots crunching on dry, compacted snow as I turned the corner.

"Too much music from the academics," I thought. "Too few Emerson transcendentalists and too many Puritanical programmers! The students need to hear inspiration from a factory furnace or a country carnival so that they might see the difference, and taste and smell the countryside. Better to understand the roar and jarring discord of the city than the polite prattling of some medieval, delicate dinner music."

As I mused over these thoughts, our course took the crowd past the side door of the concert hall, and some of the musicians were leaving. I could see the performers, wrapped in overcoats covering their black suits and dresses, struggling to get their huge bass fiddles and brass horns through the narrow causeway leading from the still-lit concert stage beyond.

How envious I was of those young musicians! My poor talents revealed in childhood that I could never become proficient in playing any instrument. Fate had marked me with a most burdensome turn of the genetic imperative—that I was to be born with a contorted left hand, totally incapable of any dexterity or strength.

At first, the aberrant fingers were a source of frustration to me, and later an embarrassment. For many years, I became quite expert in hiding the crooked limb, resorting to extremely clever and creative ways of disguising the misbegotten thing beneath sleeves and scarves and conveniently carried parcels or packages. It took half a lifetime to accept the twisted stump, and only recently had I been able to repress acute consciousness of the defect.

I suppose it really didn't matter in one respect. Apparently, the talent to learn an instrument was not there anyway, for the normal hand did little better than its unfortunate partner, no matter how long the practice. So, perhaps the physical disability was sent for a purpose, to direct me early and completely into composition, where only the mind and the pen were necessary to excel.

Life otherwise had been reasonably good to me in many respects. A chair on the faculty of the Illinois University School of Music and Composition allowed me some privileges, a reasonable salary, and a bit of time to myself. Summers could be spent traveling, and allowed the respite and room for creative composing.

In still other respects, my life was a study in isolation. Because of my infirmity, no one had found me suitable for marriage; at least I don't think such. Perhaps a built-in self-revulsion, a shame, inhibited any normal initiative I could or would have had to carry out any courting. Whatever the reasons, I lived alone in a tidy but small apartment on the North Side.

My predilection for the unusual in music and a studied contempt for all things related to money restricted my acquaintances. And although my many students and the faculty were good friends on campus, no real or long-lasting relationships had blessed my solitary path for many years.

This particular frosty night in Chicago was just another evening out alone—to hear the students perform with the professionals, to visit again my old friends, Brahms and Rachmaninoff, to revel in the familiar but timeless genius of Bach and Scarlatti. Or so I thought.

As some of the musicians joined the departing crowd down the walk, a young girl clothed in a long, dark winter coat stepped onto the path in front of me. I almost tripped trying to avoid colliding with her. "Oh, excuse me," the youngster said with her eyes cast down. I noticed she was Asian.

For a moment, she glanced quickly up at me, her hooded brown eyes furtive in the distant light of the concert hall doorway.

For that brief moment, I imagined the round and lovely face of some timeless, youthful portrait, seen a thousand times in photos and magazines, of advertisements for travel to the East. A rush of unexpected warmth emanated from that face, and although slightly startled by its presence, one could not deny it.

"Of course," I murmured, almost unheard. The group walked quietly down the campus path, only the reassuring crunch of the snow beneath our boots and the wisps of breath-steam revealing our progress.

The young girl walked directly in front of me, and I noticed for the first time that she was carrying a violin case.

Abruptly, the pathway broke into two: one to the left, to the parking lot, and one to the right, where the dormitories were.

The youngster turned to the right and started toward the dorms. I turned toward the parking lot.

"Excuse me," came a voice. It was the young violinist. She seemed to be talking to me,

"Yes," I replied. "May I help?"

"Would you walk with me to the...to the dormitories? I'm a little afraid."

"Of course," I agreed. "I would be happy to." I joined her, and looked down at her happy, innocent little face.

"Good." She affirmed. "I feel better now." And we started to walk. Soon, the soft murmur of the crowd was far behind us and the quiet, dark solitude of the deserted campus moved in around us.

"I'm glad you came tonight," she stated suddenly.

"That I came?" I asked, confused.

"Yes. I was hoping you'd come. I've been waiting," She did not look at me.

"Do I know you?" I asked.

"No, but I know you. You are Professor Danbury—you compose music and I've been waiting."

"Waiting? For what?" I could not fathom this child's conversation.

"I know you write music, and I know that you can write for the violin." She looked up with an inquisitive expression on her face.

"Why, yes—I can, and have written for the violin. Why?"

"Oh, I guess I was wondering if...if someday before...if you would write something for...for me to play." She looked at me with an expectant, somewhat apprehensive glance, then looked quickly away. The question seemed very important and yet difficult for her.

"Well, now," I replied. "Well now. That's an interesting request. Interesting, indeed." And I suppressed a smile as I glanced down at this little virtuoso walking so upright beside me.

"And would you—could you play my composition, even if it were difficult? Some of my music is very modern you know—it might seem sour and stick to your fiddle!" I warned.

"Oh, I can play your music. I already have." Her reply startled me.

"What?" I asked. But she had run ahead after thrusting her violin case into my hands.

"Oh, look! A snowman!" And she ran over to a large, malformed monster of a man made of snow, and began a mock pas de deux with him. She sang and held his broom arms and danced around and around. How alive and innocent she was! Completely engulfed in the moment, unaware of her surroundings, of the falling snow, of the night, of me. I caught up with her and watched.

"Where do you live? Aren't your parents waiting for you?" I asked, abruptly realizing that this little tyke was really unattended.

"Oh, through the park there. I'll be home pretty soon." And she skipped off down the path.

"Wait a second," I called to her. "Don't get too far ahead." The snow was swirling now, and I was beginning to worry a bit. I caught up with her again and grabbed a little mittened hand.

"Come along, young lady," and I led her along. "Incidentally, what is your name?"

"It's Sadako Asawa," she answered quickly. "You didn't ask me before, but it's Sadako Asawa. And I'm glad you're here."

"Well, I'm glad you're here too, Sadako. But we've got to get you home."

"There's no hurry," she assured me. "I'm not expected yet. But when can you write my music?" She looked up. She changed subjects so easily – a child's prerogative.

"*Your* music? So you're determined to have your piece, your sonata?" I was impressed by her persistence.

"Yes, my *sonata*! When will you do it?" Now she was excited.

"What *is* the hurry?" I asked.

She seemed to hesitate a moment and I glanced at her face. In the pale white illumination from the distant campus lights, I was astonished to see a dramatic change take place over her entire visage, as if a great, gray shadow had passed overhead and left only a pallid and frightened little child. "Because," she hesitated, "because...summer is going to...is coming, and I don't have much time." She looked at me, obviously frightened. Then she looked up to the evening sky and back at me, her little eyes wide and fearful.

"What is it, Sadako?" I asked, concerned. "What has frightened you?" And I grabbed both her arms firmly. As I did so, one of her mittens fell off, and as I stooped to gather it up, I noticed with some revulsion a large, purple ulceration on the dorsum of her hand. She quickly took the glove and put it on, holding the hand hidden in a pocket.

"Nothing." She seemed to be thinking of something far away and was not looking at me. I felt an eerie cold hand reaching through the evening air. Then she seemed to recover, and said bravely, "Really, nothing, Professor, but I must finish my practicing by summertime." Still, something in her voice.

"Why by summertime?" I asked gently, glad to see her released from her disturbing spell.

"Well, I'll have to be going home then. That's all." She said this with finality.

"Home? Where?" I was interested to know.

"Yes, home." And without elaborating, suddenly, "Do you want to hear a poem?"

"All right," I replied, dropping the more important discussion, wondering where her imagination would take her now.

"I've traveled over rolling sea,
How I came a mystery.
My ship was launched from burning shore,
Banished thenceforth evermore,
And could not sail back 'cross that sea,
Until that day I looked on Thee."

What a strange choice for a little girl, however precocious, I thought to myself. Where had I heard it before? Its somber, sepulchral mood so out of place for a child. But while I was thinking about it, she interrupted my thoughts and said, "Remember, you have to hurry—before summertime. I have to practice a lot, and I won't have much time." She started to walk a little faster into the snow, which had begun to fall somewhat faster.

"What are you practicing?" She was running faster now—moving away from me.

"You know. The Bartòk," she shouted back.

"What Bartòk?" She was moving rapidly down the path.

"Sonata for Solo Violin. Goodnight." I wasn't sure I heard her correctly. Her little voice faded into the white background, as did she. I ran for awhile, but could not catch her. The path ended abruptly and I came out onto a friendly well-lit street with several small, cozy homes lining each side. She must be home, I thought, and after a while, I turned and walked back across the lonely campus.

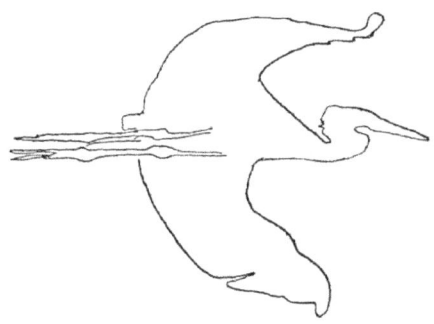

Chapter II

As I entered my apartment that evening, the warmth of the floor heater was gratefully felt. Yet, I did not consciously notice my surroundings. The recent memory of Sadako rather filled my mind. I wondered why our paths had crossed—I challenged mentally the circumstances that caused the precise timing of any meeting. They say that everything happens for some reason. I personally don't agree entirely, although certainly some events obviously are "for the best." Yet, how does one explain the chance meetings that result in tragedy? The car crushed by a truck in the middle of nowhere, at some desolate juncture in Time that only Fate could have planned. Are our experiences preordained toward a foregone end? Can anyone prove that nasty and redoubtable theory of Predestination? Certainly not to my satisfaction.

I must confess that my first and continuing impulse was to project a pessimistic, blackly negative image as the underriding basis or predominant hue of my life.

After all, the majority of the human experience is one of deprivation and self-discipline to prepare for something better; of pain and exertion to realize something accomplished; of anticipation and anxiety before almost everything that produces elation. And after every elation, there must be some type of falling off, of a lessening of the joy, of a dilution of the love, or partial regret after victory, of sadness after that precious meeting; there must be, by the nature of any sentient, quasi-intelligent being, a period of resolving activity, of diminishing emotion, of relaxing tensions after every climax. It cannot be otherwise, this dénouement.

Sad to say, it is the vastness of emptiness of those periods of compensatory action and emotions, their depth and extremes, which contribute most profoundly to and comprise principally the total negative burden through which one can either function or rally, or under which he is eventually crushed. Such were my empty times without someone or something to touch-to communicate with.

Yet, little Sadako and I *had* met that evening. I had uncharacteristically broken through my long worn mantle of detachment, and had overtly opened a door.

And through that door had passed a small, strange figure.

As I poured a little milk into a bowl, I thought, "An interesting child, that one. Imagine! Her own sonata! Presumptuous little imp." I wondered how well she played. Probably very well, to be working on the Bartòk. But something bothered me—what had Sadako said about Bartòk? Solo violin? I don't think so. Bartòk, to my knowledge, had written no such piece.

I could not have known it then, that it would be several years after Bartòk's death before the music world learned of that score, commissioned late in his life. He continued to work on it even to his death on September 26, 1945. He died of leukemia. In 1945....1945.

I opened the window to the fire escape leading from my third floor apartment. As I placed the milk on the outside ledge, the large gray Tom spit at me with ears lowered, and the orange and black female lowered her ears and warned me with her high-pitched, low-volume growl. Several ragged looking kittens cowered and skittered in the background, doing their usual remarkable balancing act between stairs and porch and ledge. And as I reached out to pet the female, she spit and snarled and leaped sideways into the darkness. Discouraged but not surprised, I pulled back in.

But before I could close the window, a lithe little black and white form shot past me and alighted on the kitchen floor, and sat there on the kitchen floor, with dainty little white feet, and an ebony back, and a comical black mask over a little white underjaw.

And this tiny little creature looked up at me—unafraid. I stooped slowly to pick her up, expecting a quick rebuke. Instead, she leaned into my hand and grew limp as I lifted her. I placed her on my lesser hand to observe her more closely.

How soft you are, I thought—and why so friendly? Who are you and where are you from? Did someone send you from a distance just to visit? Or is there a message? Surely, a message! But you're cold and wet—Are you hungry?—Yes, of course you are.

And I took some scraps from the icebox and fed them to my little visitor. She ate and drank hungrily. Yet, when I picked her up again, she remained completely tame and gentle, purring softly on my arm.

We had met and we were friends.

And we spent that first evening together, she content to lie with her head up and eyes closed, pressed against my leg, and I listening to the radio concert and reading, my truncated hand resting on her tiny form as I fell gradually into a light sleep.

And for some reason, ghostly dreams of distant fields and strange tidal pools and estuaries crossed dimly in my mind. And I was distracted by unstructured visions of snow and city lights, and of a large choir singing voicelessly before an empty stadium.

And the cutting wind outside bore endlessly against the rattling windows, reminding me, even in sleep, that security and warmth and friendship and life are shielded for only a moment from the wiles of Time and Nature, and then are gone forever. And with these thoughts, I fell into a deep slumber....

Shut in from all the world without,
Content to let the North Wind roar
in baffled rage at pane and door.
   Whittier.
   "Snow Bound"

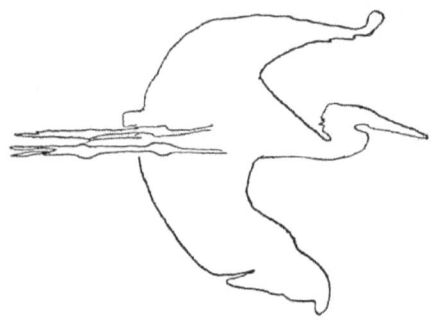

Chapter III

The next day came borne on sunny skies. As I walked briskly toward my office, hands in pockets, I reflected cheerfully on the campus crowd. Young people on their way to class, all bundled up like little soldiers on their way to meet another day's challenge. The sounds of laughter and excited talk echoed across the frosted lawns—each with some message of hope or anticipation, of last evening's adventures, of plans for tonight—there was no place for gloom among these young people.

Strange, thought I. Yesterday was just another drab moment in my life; but today—I was buoyant, weightless. I felt a strong kinship with these happy young people. Why? What made to-day so different? I mused contentedly as I approached the Performing Arts Center.

As I passed the building, I heard the distinct disharmony of students practicing and performing in different study rooms. This atonality was strangely appealing to me, but always had been a source of some confusion.

Why weren't these rooms completely sound-proofed? Surely, it was not beyond the technology of the time to confine each room's melody to within its own parameters.

Yet there it was: the polytonal fugue of brass and voice, of violin and piano, of flute and snare—all producing that distinct unstructured symphony of sounds, sounds that only the revolutionary Ives, I believed, had listened to, understood, and utilized in so many of his thorny masterpieces. Only Ives had the courage, honesty and creative genius to put it all together. Like the tumultuous clamor of a crowd in a subway station mixing with the racket and din of the approaching train, he knew that those disparate sounds, seemingly unrelated, were truly closely linked and bound together to produce a total entity. What seemed chaos to others was simply and naturally music to him. And to those who complained that his sounds didn't seem right—too loud, too complex, too—unmusical—Ives would explode, "My God! What has sound got to do with music!?!"

And I thought to myself, if only his genius could be loaned to me for a short while— couldn't I produce even a short piece to compare with his?

A short piece, a song or an etude. Or a sonata. A *sonata*! Of course! And coincidentally with this abrupt reminder that I had, indeed, some work to do, the riveting sound of a violin pierced the dry, cold air around me. Through all the dim cacophony came a sound so pure and different from the rest, I stopped abruptly to listen.

Several stories up this old and weathered stone building, a window was open. And from that source came the exquisite tones of an instrument played with great eloquence. As I listened to that elegiac paean, at once majestic and mournful, I realized that it was strangely familiar, yet consciously unknown to me. It seemed as though I knew it well, and could anticipate each phrase before it came, *but I had never heard it before!*

For several minutes that haunting lament filled my ears and my mind. No distraction or other sound could penetrate my momentary preoccupation. And then with a start, I knew immediately and instinctively that it was Sadako.

I looked up toward that dark window and, as I did, the music ceased. There appeared at the window a young, round face. I could hardly make out the features at such a distance, and for some reason, (there seemed to be a mist around that part of the building—perhaps snow-steam from an over-heated radiator pipe), the face was made indistinct.

She looked down, and I waved excitedly to her. She hesitated, lifted her hand for only a second— then turned quickly and was gone.

Had she seen me? Was it Sadako?

But now the music was gone as well, and after a long wait, I continued on my way. With an unexplained feeling of sadness, I glanced back once more at that building and its dark window, but no one was there. And somehow, I instinctively knew that to search for her would have been hopeless.

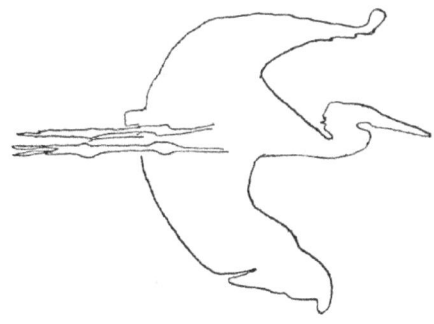

Chapter IV

It was several more weeks before I saw Sadako again. As a matter of fact, I had tried to locate her at the music school, where special classes for gifted younger students were held, but it was semester break and no one was around to answer questions. One young student happened by, but told me that she didn't know of Sadako or anyone of her description. She was only a freshman, she went on, and knew very few other students.

Was Sadako a student? Or a "visitor," a part-time special registrant? How little I knew of her. In fact, all I knew about her was what little information she had shared on that first evening after the concert. What was it she had said about summer coming? And something about time....

As I contemplated my ineptness, I heard a call from across the campus lawn. I had been walking back to my car at the end of a long, but productive day. The students had shown more interest than usual in my lecture, and seemed to really want to know more about the composer-subject of the day. Was the man's life really interesting, or had I made it *seem* interesting? I must say that my presentations seemed to have more vitality of late—and I couldn't deny my refound pleasure in bringing my thoughts and research and, yes, opinions to the students.

The violin sonata was taking form. Progress was easier than it had been. Single notes became whole phrases—the central theme began to take on a life of its own—wandering through the work, becoming vague and subtle at times, and bold and prominent at others.

At any rate, that call broke through these thoughts, and I turned. Unconsciously, I smiled at the waving figure, then started back toward her.

"Sadako, my word! Where have you been?!"

"Oh, I've been gone a while." She repressed a smile." And how are you?" Her face was shining, her black hair lightly dampened by a gentle snowfall. She was dressed in a little blue schoolgirl skirt with white knee socks. Yet, she was not the little girl I had walked with last January. Something had changed. Could I have misjudged her age on that dark evening?

"Very well, very well," unable to disguise the pleasure in my voice.

"And the sonata—my sonata?" Her eyes were animated, her voice colored with a young girl's anticipation. Strangely, she seemed more poised, much more mature than last time.

"*Your* sonata! You remember that?" I laughed.

"Yes, of course I do," she answered me.

"I have been working on it, and it is going well."

"When will you finish it?" she asked excitedly.

"I'm not sure—I have a few revisions to make and one section is not going well."

"The adagio!"

"How in heaven's name did you know that?! Yes, the adagio."

"Oh, it's always the slowest part that's the most difficult." She began to lecture me in all seriousness. "People think that the heroic, exciting parts are the hardest to compose and perform, but it's really the slower, gentler moments that are the most difficult to master. It seems that it's harder to be gentle and tender than strong and commanding. There is an old Asian saying that 'gentleness is strength.' It has always been so. Time cannot change that." And she seemed to be looking off at something far away. Suddenly, she became self-conscious, blushed, and laughed a little at the last, a young girl's laugh.

"Yes, it is nearing completion. I need only some little stimulus to guide me to the end."

"What could be your stimulus?" she wondered aloud, looking away.

"Why not you?" I asked, amusedly misreading her coquettish handling of the question.

"Oh, no! Not me! I'm not anybody. I'm not important enough to be your inspiration."

"My *inspiration*! That's the word! Good girl. You *will* be my inspiration. Perhaps you have been all along." I laughed at her worried little face.

"Oh, no! It cannot be me. I am just a student. Please don't think of me in that way. You know so many important people. I was thinking, well— perhaps Ives would be the one."

"Ives? You know about Ives?" I looked at her wise little face. But of course you do, I thought.

"Oh, well, *always* Ives. He inspires everything I do. But important people? Well, yes, I know many, but not one I know has inspired me."

"But how have *you* been?" I asked, quickly diverting the conversation. "How are your studies going?"

"Very well, thank you," she replied." We're doing the Sibelius this Christmas."

"The Sibelius Violin Concerto? Yes, I know. What a glorious work. Isn't it a shame that it isn't done more often?"

"Yes." She seemed to be thinking of something.

"And who is the soloist?" I asked gently. Surely not her, however accomplished. There were so many professionals around.

"John Mallory. He's very good, Oh, he's really wonderful!"

"Ah yes, Mallory. Yes, he's excellent, though I know he prefers Brahms. Why didn't they choose you, my young Heifetz?"

"Me? As soloist? Oh, I'm not nearly good enough for that!" She blushed and tried to hide a smile....

"Really?!" I asked. "And how can you tell me that, after I heard you playing last month?" I watched her face carefully, looking for some sign or change.

"You heard me?" She looked at me, then away, nervously.

"Yes, my young student, and you were wonderful! What was that piece you were playing? It sounded like something I had heard, yet I didn't recognize it."

"Are you sure it was I who was playing?"

"Come new, you waved at me from your practice room. You surely saw me there, waving to you from the street below."

"But the window to my practice room is sealed. It is a very old building, you know, so some of those windows can't be opened."

"What? But one surely *was* open. And someone, you, I thought, was playing some magnificent composition up there. And then you waved—at least someone waved."

"I'm afraid you are mistaken." She said this glumly, almost sadly.

"I wonder who it was," I said, with disappointment in my voice.

I tried to look at her, but she avoided my gaze.

"The piece she was playing—can you re-member it?" she asked suddenly.

"Most certainly. I will never forget it, at least part of it."

"Will you hum it?"

"Of course." And I began humming the melody for her, trying to remember each interval and note. But before I could finish, Sadako joined with me and we hummed the last four bars in unison.

"You *have* played that piece," I demanded, almost angrily.

"It seems I, too, have heard it before." She appeared disturbed, then preoccupied, as though she was listening to some far-off orchestra playing that haunting theme—somewhere very far away.

"You *have* heard it! Who is it? Who is the composer, little professor?"

"I...I don't know. I don't remember where I heard it. It just seems to be there." She gazed past me, at nothing at all.

"Someday I will find the source of that exquisite piece. Perhaps you will help me," I suggested.

"Perhaps," she replied gravely, but she seemed to be thinking of something else, or listening to something I could not hear.

"You play very well, you know."

"Can you be sure?" she asked.

"Yes," I replied firmly," I am sure."

"Oh." Again, her eyes were cast down, and then, somewhat reluctantly," I'm afraid I'd better go now."

"But it's semester break."

"I'm doing extra work for credits. I'd better run." She reached out her hand. My withered hand had been carefully concealed in the extra car blanket I carried around in winter. I had reached out my normal hand, but she avoided it and grasped the blanket and its contents. I pulled back, embarrassment crossing my face. I tried to pull away, but she pressed my poor withered hand even more firmly.

"Goodbye, Professor," she said with an earnestness that disarmed me. She smiled as warm a smile as I have ever seen, and then was gone.

For a long time, I stood there on the quiet, deserted campus ground. The wind became more icy, and the snowflakes began to sting my cheeks. But the lingering memory, the tactile sense of that firm, reassuring grip stayed on.

She knew, I thought. She knew so much. Indeed, how much of life *did* she know? And how could one so young be so wise and understanding?

The sound of the theme followed me home that evening, and I could not forget her little humming voice....

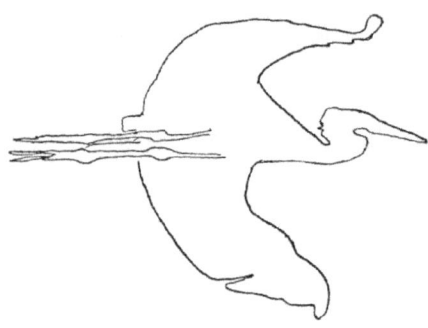

Chapter V

In a small French village near Enghien Les Bain, an aging schoolmaster sat quietly and watched the expressions of his young students. He keenly observed their faces as they grasped for the answer to his question.

As an old friend of Professor Danbury from their days at the University of Chicago so many years ago, he frequently complained to Charles in letters that at no time was he satisfied that his philosophical teachings were understood or accepted by his students. If only someday he could retire to his loft, knowing that his life's efforts had succeeded in opening the doors of civility and love to them. Then and only then, could he close his eyes to rest – indeed, to sleep.

He addressed the students, "What would you give to each and every individual of the world to make him or her perfectly happy, if only for a moment – yet knowing that you would perish in a wisp the second that gift was given? Would you do it? And why?"

The first student, a bright young fellow with quick eyes, first offered a solution. "I would, of course, not consider such a thought, for it is purely theoretical, not practical, and in the end, obliterative. Quite impossible and ridiculous!"

"A clever and useful answer," replied the teacher. "Yet in refusing to answer my question, you deny yourself the excitement of experiencing, if only for a moment, some-thing foreign to you – another's happiness."

A second student, a handsome young girl, sug-gested this: "I would give everyone the means to raise a family, own a house, and be domestically secure. Yet, I hesitate to tell you, this is only a thought, for I cannot imagine giving up myself to make others happy. I mean, to ask that sacrifice would be so presumptuous and final!"

"Agreed," said the little professor. "So presumptuous a demand of one so young and beautiful – with so much of her life ahead."

"Wealth," stated a tall, bespectacled student with thick curly hair and an aquiline proboscis."Wealth could buy one everything and thus is the only gift to give. Of course, to expect one to perish for another's satisfaction is preposterous and naïve. Surely the question belies a sensible answer." His ever moist palms were even more moist as he spoke.

"Power!" stated a gaunt, blue-eyed young woman with twitching fingers and a nervous tic." Power over her life – and, indeed, over the lives of others. Only so could she enjoy true satisfaction and be content in the realization that no one could control her life or her thoughts. But to cease to exist so that other might enjoy what one desires herself is ludicrous and self-defeating. Absurd!"

"Honest and revealing answers," nodded the professor to the last two respondents.

And one by one, the students gave their choices of gifts to those theoretical and unbodied souls proffered by their teacher. Beauty, intelligence, insight, wisdom – all were excellent suggestions. No one, however, would accept the Terminal Requirement, and no answer satisfied the elder.

He looked about for more. At that moment, he espied a plain, sad girl, sitting in the back of the classroom, gazing out at the autumnal garden. She seemed not to hear what was occurring about her.

"And you, young dreamer," said the teacher. "What is your answer?"

For some moments, no reply came, and a nearby student jostled the young woman's arm to gain her attention and interrupt her reverie.

"Oh, please, sir. I have no wish to offer my poor thoughts on your question. My answer would surely seem ludicrous and too simple to you. Please do not request my answer."

And her pale, unpretty Asian face seemed uncommonly wan in the reflection of the golden sun from without.

"Nonsense, my young student. Your answer is as valid as the next. Perhaps you can awaken this august group with something different." And his blue eyes gleamed with interest.

"Please, sir. My answer – my solution – is too simple!"

The professor responded quietly and with great gentleness: "Yet, I command you to reply."

"If I must, then please forgive my most inconsequential thoughts." She began, slowly and thoughtfully. "It seems that the most important and greatest gift I might give to everyone, that they might possess great and perfect happiness, would be no more than to provide them with a moment of perfect love within and perfect love returned. Untethered by constraint or doubt, this love would entail absolute regard, one for another, and none for oneself. This love would transcend the shared love of a mother with her child. For the child's love is parasitic and contains no voluntary side. The child takes as the mother provides. No, this given love should be be-tween equals in all senses of the word. Thus would all other distractions be unnoticed, indeed, nonexistent. And their happiness would be of such completeness as to make the lovers as one in the most spiritual of designs."

The professor's eyes glistened. "Hear you, O students! This fair maiden would give naught of tangible goods, as you, but of the most ephemeral of habiliments. Can you not see the perfection of her choice? For after your given moment of happiness had passed, those whose losses were of wealth or power or beauty, the most earthly of human artifacts, those poor players would be left with an empty nothingness and sad regrets, but no substitutes.

For those whose gift this young dreamer gives, there would be forever the undiminishable memory of perfection felt and of the complete fulfillment of all human need for Happiness, our goal today."

Turning to the girl, the professor gently asked, with a quiet voice and a faint smile, the final question: "And would you, my fair dreamer, accept as the Ultimate Contract your own eternal demise as the balance in the trade?"

He watched her intently, and with the wisdom of his years, he felt her heart's response, and with it, his journey's end.

She turned from him and looked again to the garden. Her face was now glowing with a strange radiance, not from the garden, but from some deeper source within. There was a touch of timeless sadness and resignation in her voice, and her misty eyes looked far be-yond the blooms. Her reply was expressed as the gentlest of sighs, yet everyone heard:

"Without hesitation."

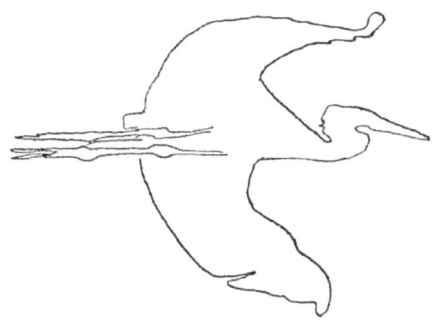

Chapter VI

Thanksgiving was just a memory, as Christmas with all its color descended on Chicago. We were blessed by an abundant snowfall, and the city rejoiced in its new white mantle. Children played in the parks, and large throngs of shoppers marched happily through shopping malls.

Michigan Avenue was brilliantly illuminated as one fine, cold, dry evening I was doing my annual window shopping. For a brief moment, the world, embroiled in its most destructive war, was forgotten. The turbulence overseas seemed far away and unreal.

We could not have anticipated the approaching cataclysm.

How, indeed, could we, safely separated from the grime and blood, comprehend the pain? Too far to see—so far to feel. The muffled gunfire, the screeching "steel hawks," the screaming dead and dying—too far to feel. How, indeed, to know the utter desolation of a blinded boy, a dismembered infantryman, a suddenly childless mother, the collapsed and mutilated remains of her child hanging from her anguished arms as she holds it to the incandescent sky?!

No—surrounded and immersed in the celebration of the moment, we could not comprehend the agony.

I wondered with the wide-eyed children at gigantic displays, with their enormous, twinkling Santas and his reindeer, at those marvelously clever little trains, and at Christmas trees brightly lit in every color imaginable: white trees and green trees and red trees! What great fun! And I quickly lost myself in the easy, happy memories of childhood sojourns with my family, remembering those happy pathways where we went, but could not go again.

Times and circumstances had changed, and I now had no one to walk with. I was becoming accustomed to these solitary forays into the

Christmas fantasy. I didn't really *feel* alone, though, for there was always the laughter and vitality and enthusiastic infatuation of the children. They swept us all along, and the moment was as it had always been: pure magic!

I turned the corner, followed the happy legion to the west, and was examining closely an animated elf when a reflection in the window caught my eye. A lovely round visage peered in from the crowd behind me. I recognized the face immediately and spun around.

"Sadako!" I called. At first she did not seem to hear, and she turned to continue down the walk.

"Sadako!" I shouted again. She stopped and turned. She seemed to hesitate, then smiled sweetly.

"Professor Danbury. How good to see you!" She came toward me. As she held out her hand, I noticed with an unseen start that she appeared pale and tired. And, remarkably, much taller—no longer the adolescent.

"Hello, Sadako, how are you? Have you been busy with your studies?"

"Oh, yes," she answered. "Very busy."

"And your violin—is practice going well?"

"Yes. I'm progressing slowly but surely," her usual self-deprecating response.

"But surely you are studying too much. You look pale to me. Are you well?"

"Oh, yes," she quickly answered me. "I'm perfectly fine. I guess I don't get much sun at this time of year," she said with a little laugh.

"Tell me about your studies. What are you working on now? I am most interested in your progress. You know that, don't you?"

"Yes," she answered softly, this time with eyes cast downward.

"Then tell me!" I took her arm and we walked slowly with the crowd.

"Well, you know the Sibelius. It is going well. Mr. Mallory is really marvelous—oh, he can make the violin sing!"

As can you, I thought to myself.

"The third movement is very difficult, very technical and demanding, as you know."

"Yes, I know."

"But the orchestra sounds wonderful—we will be performing on New Year's Day."

"Yes. I am planning to attend."

"And I...I have begun working on a special project." She seemed reluctant to bring up the subject.

"Good girl! What is it?" But I already suspected.

"I did a little research and found some copies of Ives' Third Violin Sonata."

"Ah ha! I thought so! And?"

"And so, I have begun studying it, though it seems so difficult."

"How did this all begin?" I asked, wondering how she would answer.

"Well, you being so involved with his works, after hearing your thoughts and talks-being so...so concentric with his life and compositions, I began to review what we had available at the library."

"As I reviewed some copies of his Third Symphony, I found a more solemn and gentle timbre than he wrote into his other works. And the Third Sonata seems to parallel that symphony. Besides, the others are so technically demanding that I knew I could never do them justice."

"Nonsense. But good thinking anyway. Have you started working with the violin?"

"Yes, a little, but I am reading more about the man to understand his work."

"An excellent plan. There is much about him few people know."

But before I could go on, "Oh, look!" she cried. "Candied apples—my favorite! Could we have one?"

"Of course." I looked hard at her, but she refused to return my gaze, and instead tugged me over to the apple stand. Two sticky apples later, we walked quietly down a quiet section of the mall. Snow had begun to fall, just as it always seemed to when I was around Sadako.

> They hand in hand, with
> wandering step and slow,
> Through Eden took their
> solitary way....
> Milton —
> *Paradise Lost*
> Book XII

"Do you feel comfortable?" I asked quietly.

"Oh yes." Her tone was warm.

"I mean, with me."

"That *is* what I mean." She spoke in lowered tones, and something in her voice conveyed a deeper reply.

"I must say that each time I have met you, I experience a strange combination of security and warmth—something I have done without for many years."

"I, too, feel what you feel. It is good, and it makes me feel a deep happiness." Her words thus stated surprised me. She spoke in a strangely foreign way, and I again envisioned that timeless Asian face before me.

"Yet, we are not together, Sadako. I never see you, though I must admit, you are in my thoughts many times each day. At first, I ignored whatever role you could possibly play in my life, solitary as it has been. You, the student, bright and fresh, I the professor, wizened and cynical. What could possibly come of such a disparate pair? Perhaps in another time and another place, we...I mean if you had come sooner, much sooner, there might have been *some* reasonable...." I hesitated to go on. How *could* she have come sooner?

"But why," I smiled, "would one so lovely and young spend any time or energy on a crippled...."

"You are *not* a cripple!" She spoke quickly and looked hard at me.

"But I am, sadly so."

"You are complete, Professor Danbury. There is no part of you which is not complete." With that, she took my arm and held it firmly. Strangely put, I thought. But no other words, however said, could have meant as much to me.

For a while, we walked silently in the snow.

"You truly mean what you say, don't you?" I asked gently.

"I say to you as I would say to myself," she said firmly. Again, strangely phrased, yet the perfect answer. We walked on for some distance.

How do you do it, Sadako, I thought to myself. How do you, confined as you are in that youthful temple, manage to embrace the faults, the artifacts, the aging me, the unclear future, the unknown why and how and when, as if you somehow were Nature Herself, neither acknowledging nor condemning aberrations from perfection?

And then, aloud, "You seem to be, at once, the ideal—the perfect companion—and, at the same time, the embodiment of that Great Genetrix we all instinctively seek."

"Please, do not say 'perfect' when you speak of me. I, more than anyone, am imperfect!"

"Impossible! Can you explain, then, this capacity of yours to make me feel whole for the first time in my life?"

But Sadako ignored the question and said, instead, "We have come to the subway—-I must say goodbye." She turned. Suddenly, she started to shiver and she looked at me, obviously disturbed by something. "I hate subways—they frighten me so, all the noise, and...." She was rubbing the top of her mittened hand.

"My car is not far," I said, knowing the answer.

"Please, no, thank you. I must catch the next train. There is studying to do tonight, and...."

"Yes, I know, Sadako. I know. And as you go, can you tell me when we'll meet? At school—at the concert? I know you *cannot* tell me."

"What do you mean? Why do you say that?"

"I think you know, Sadako. You will reappear when it is time, for whatever purpose that you do return, and until you come, where will you be? Can you tell me?"

"I hear my train. Goodbye, dear Professor Danbury." She touched my arm and turned.

I did not try to stop her. Then, remembering something, "Sadako, before you go, one question."

"Yes?"

I struggled with my memories of the very young girl of only a few months ago, and with the vision of this young lady receding before me.

"Never mind. Go now, and be happy ...and—come back."

"I...I'll try." She turned and hurried off, and I turned back into that peculiar cold that turns the city air from dry and brisk to damp and biting. That peculiar cold that penetrates deep into one's very soul.

The melancholy days are come,
the saddest of the year.

"Death of the Flowers"
William Cullen Bryant

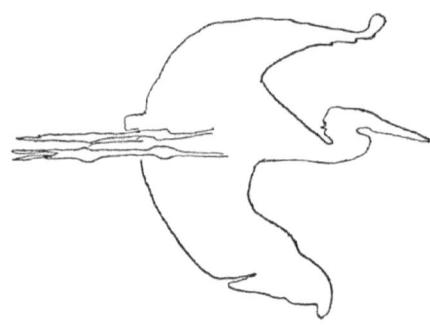

Chapter VII

I did not see Sadako again that winter. As often as I passed that dark window, I never again heard those vibrant sounds, but then, I didn't expect to. As it turned out, Sadako was not registered as a student at all, but, remembering her words outside the concert hall so long ago, she was "visiting." Perhaps as an exchange student— but from where, I thought, knowing I would not find out, at least not from her.

My sonata was essentially completed. Only a portion of the adagio remained, but its substance continued to escape me. As hard as I tried, the form and structure evaded materialization, and only the haunting theme reappeared over and over again, played in some misty garden by an unseen artist, and, yes, on a seraphic, unearthly violin.

The campus bushes and trees were beginning to blossom in the spring thaw. Small birds and burrowing animals were in more evidence now, and the grass had that special smell that reminds one of those endless childhood memories.

I was making plans to spend a month in Los Angeles that summer. My research and lectures had been arranged for me and, this year, I would see California for the first time.

"Looking forward to the summer, Charles?" Leon Benson asked. Leon was an old friend, the only member of the faculty who seemed to understand and support my penchant for modern music, for the avant garde—my dedication to the works of Bartòk and Ives. As a conductor, his seniority allowed him a certain degree of autonomy, and he chose his programs with little fear of objection.

"Of course, Leon. Can't wait. Imagine living all these years and not having visited the West Coast!"

"Incidentally, Charles, any more information on Sadako? I haven't heard you mention her lately." His eyes had a quizzical look to them. Leon had been the only person to whom I had mentioned my strange meeting with Sadako, and I was somewhat surprised that he had remembered her name, let alone the incident.

"Not a thing, Leon. She's like a ghost. Here for a moment, surrounded by a seemingly endless snowy mist, and then she's gone. To where, I don't know."

"I see," Leon seemed to be contemplating something.

"The reason I ask is that...well, something unusual occurred last week which reminded me of Sadako."

"What could that be?" My curiosity was immediately aroused.

"Well, it might be nothing, but...well, I may have bumped into another...another 'Sadako' in Wisconsin."

"What in heaven's name do you mean?" I sat forward, immediately alert, my interest piqued.

"Well, it seemed rather odd, but as you know, I was guest conductor at Marquette University last Thursday evening. I have always enjoyed that young group. Only a few really talented students, but all really quite involved and enthusiastic."

"Well, what happened?" I was beginning to feel that unseen hand reaching out.

"As you know, I rehearse the orchestra on Wednesday evening, before the Thursday night performance. Their own conductor has usually whipped them into pretty acceptable shape."

"Yes?"

"And as I went over the Sibelius...."

"Sibelius? The Violin Concerto?" I held my breath.

"Yes, how did you know? Oh, I must have mentioned it."

No, you didn't, I remarked to myself.

"At any rate, the soloist was a tall, striking Asian girl. Kind of odd, like some coincidence— you with your Sadako in Chicago, and now this student in Wisconsin."

"Go on," I said, holding my breath.

"Couldn't have been Sadako, though. Her name was Akemi."

"Why on earth would you think she and Sadako were somehow—related?" I was puzzled.

"Well, it's hard to say. But as we were re- viewing the score to the last movement—and, incidentally, she played the Sibelius magnificently—she kept mentioning Bartòk and Ives and how her next projects would include their works. And she talked rather dreamily, I would say, almost trance-like, about some future day when she would perform some great modern works by *another* man."

"Not *that* unusual, Leon. Some of the students see the value of the modernists, although I do agree that there is a slight coincidence." I was looking for something else.

"That's not it, Charles. This is where it really gets confusing, and not a little, well—disturbing." He hesitated.

"Yes, go on, please!"

"The evening of the concert, she was very nervous. I thought I understood why, but she said no, not the usual pre-performance jitters. No—something more profound was disturbing her."

"For heaven's sake, Leon, what?!?"

"It seems that she had had a premonition or, more accurately, a flashback to another time—another place. She could see and near herself playing a most wondrous piece of music. It was like nothing else she had ever heard. She felt that this music, with its overpoweringly beautiful theme, was so real that she was afraid it would interfere with her present performance, and that she would *not* be able to play the Sibelius. And what's more...."

I interrupted him, anticipating the rest.

"She saw herself playing in a small room on the fifth floor of a building on our campus."

"More, Charles." Leon was looking at me intensely.

"More? I can't imagine what else...."

"*You* were the composer!"

"I?!" I asked, astonished.

"By name, Charles, you!"

"But I've never met the girl. I've never been to that campus. And I surely don't remember any student that fits that description. I am sure I would remember her!"

"I know, I know," said Leon. "Yet she named the composer, the place. It's all too confusing."

"And the theme! Did she play it for you?" I was impatient and excited beyond belief.

"She played a little of it on her violin. And, Charles...."

"Yes?"

"It was magnificent, rhapsodic, unearthly. It was at once the apogee of all the lyrical music written for the violin, compounded and reduced into one concentrated mass of musical energy. It was breathtakingly and violently beautiful. I cannot tell you what a disturbing effect that music had on me! I later found myself listening to that theme even as I conducted the Sibelius. I could not shake it from my head. I actually feared that I would lose my way and ruin the concert for that young lady and her orchestra."

"But you didn't?"

"No. It went well. She played magnificently, perfectly. Emotionally mature, wonderfully poised, technically a wonder. She played with great dignity—and yet...." He seemed suddenly to be reviewing something in his mind's eye. His eyes widened.

"Yes?"

"That's strange. Now that I think of it, she performed the piece *completely* differently than she had at rehearsal. With much greater warmth, strangely but beautifully different phrasing. Not anything like her earlier performance. *As though two different people had performed on two different nights!"* He suddenly looked at me in amazement. "Charles—what was it?"

"No, Leon—not 'what was it,' but 'who was she?' I do not know. I am even more confused now. I have no explanation or even rational thoughts on this matter. I must sit and think a bit. Would you excuse me?" I suddenly felt limp and exhausted. No reasonable explanation or even a lucid thought was possible at that moment. I was looking numbly at the floor.

"If it will help, I will leave you this." Leon placed some musical manuscripts on the piano. "They're all I can remember of that confounded theme. I should be able to have given you the whole thing but for some reason, beyond a certain point, my memory becomes hazy and the music obscure. As though some great, ghostly hand reaches out to stop my writing or remembering— for what reason, I cannot guess. Goodbye, Charles. I will check on you later. If I can be of any help, anything, let me know." This last he said gently, and then quietly retreated from the room, closing the door silently behind him.

My hand rested on the manuscript for a long while. I knew long before I opened it that the score Leon had left contained my theme, note for note—unaltered—just as I had written it months before.

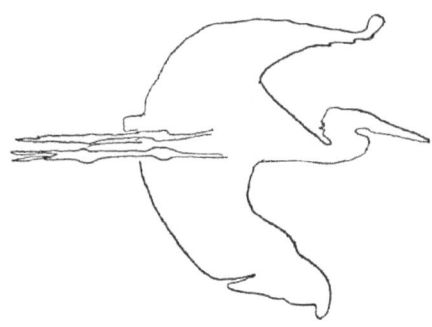

Chapter VIII

It was the last week in June. The train ride from Chicago to Los Angeles had been relaxing. The Super Chief was wonderful, all silver and modern, smooth as a pond even at high speeds, as I sat nestled in that great windowed observation car.

What an enormous land this is, I had thought. Three days and nights to cross its vast expanses. How could one see so much in so short a time? Should it not take a lifetime or a hundred lifetimes to span such a land? Crossing in moments what took the settlers months—-bizarre landscapes of sky pink and muck gray. Where now, the cowboys—the buffalo—the Kiowas and Comanches? Gone—all gone. A land stripped bare of any animate inhabitants, left to bake in the mirthless Sun—a raw, parched animal hide, stretched out, all wrinkled and furrowed with variegated pastel rocks holding down the curling edges.

Then, on past sapphire lakes and deep canyons lined by imprisoned Douglas firs, forever reaching up to that wisp of blue sky above for a fleeting touch of a passing sunray.

How far away the University, Chicago and the students seemed— how tiny they all became when thrown in contrast against these great valleys and mountains. The city with its cold and sodden and noisy streets, towering buildings, and great river became but an insignificant, if raucous, speck, lost against these great and silent brooding expanses. Our silver serpentine stagecoach rushed on, a singular and lonely anachronism in a timeless, prehistoric domain.

Once in Los Angeles, it took some time and a long bus ride to my hotel to remind me that as large as Chicago was, Los Angeles was more expansive. Lodging was adequate, if not luxurious. I was traveling, of course, on a university budget, and expected little superfluity.

The hotel was located not far from the University campus, and across the street from a delightful little grassy park. I studied the park from my fifth floor window and could see that it was actually fairly large, encompassing several blocks to the south and east of the hotel. Trees of all sorts grew randomly along several little gravel paths, and I marveled at the variety of foliage supported by this temperate climate.

Several benches were scattered about, and occasionally I saw an old person or two resting on them, gazing contentedly at some flowering bush, as if renewing some old memory of better times past.

One evening, upon returning to my room after a productive day at the music library, I leaned on the windowsill and studied the scene below.

It was nearing sunset and golden, broken rays of light cut through the trees in the park below. Traffic was strangely nonexistent on that Sunday evening—travelers and workers home by then for dinner and a warm respite from the day's chores, I supposed.

For some reason, I suddenly decided to explore the park—it was still light, and I wasn't really very hungry yet.

I wrapped my ever present scarf around my neck, remembering warnings by other travelers that evenings in Los Angeles could be quite chilly, and hurried down to the lobby.

I crossed the street and entered the park without encountering a single car or pedestrian. Remarkably quiet and peaceful, I thought—how relaxing.

I ventured from the grassy lawns into the deeper forest-like spaces beyond. At first, the seclusion afforded by those trees was somewhat eerie, not a little foreboding, but the warm wind, not yet turned cold by the advancing dusk, and the songs of countless birds urged me on.

As I walked down one long, shadowed narrow path, I heard the sounds of something striking periodically against a wall or fence.

"Hmm," I thought. "The last of the young people playing catch, or tennis, or something. A bit late, it seems."

I pushed through a final group of low-lying magnolia branches and came upon a small glade.

Unnoticed by me at the time, the bird songs had faded away. No insects chirped or buzzed.

Centered within the glade, a tall, rectangular, narrow concrete wall stood starkly erect, a somewhat unpleasant artifact in this lovely glen. Its proportions were reminiscent of something in my dim memory—vague, dark, strongly disturbing—an unfocused shadow somewhere in time.

It was then I saw the little girl. She was throwing a tennis ball with great effort and enthusiasm at the wall, then running quickly after it as it rebounded back. Her clothes looked rather dusty and old.

She had the delightfully discoordinated movements of most young children, all elbows and knees and legs, flailing about, stumbling, laughing, encouraging herself aloud all the while. Her white knee socks had fallen to her ankles. She was Asian.

I looked around for her guardian. No one was there. She stooped to pick up her straw hat and adjusted it on her head.

"Hello," she said cheerfully. "I'm glad you came."

"Hello," I replied, somewhat uneasily. "Are you having a good time?" still looking for some companion. The circumstances were eerily reminiscent.

"Oh, yes! This is fun!" she squealed breathlessly, and chased after a particularly errant rebound. The ball skittered past me and I unconsciously reached out with my amorphous hand, recovering quickly enough to retrieve the ball with the normal one. I threw it back to her, searching her little face for any revealing expressions. Apparently, she had not seen. I certainly did not want to frighten this little lonely waif. Every once in a while, she would stop to brush off her little navy blue skirt. It was then that I noticed her face—and drew in a quick breath.

Subtle shadows and tossing hair almost disguised what I knew immediately were the unmistakable features of a sightless left eye. Her little pageboy hairstyle reaffirmed what I already knew. A blotchy sore defiled her left cheek.

"Thanks," she said, catching the ball awkwardly. She went back to her solitary game.

"Where are your parents?" I asked.

"Oh, they're not here. They live far away," She didn't look up, but continued her game.

"Where is far away?"

"Amache, I think. They're in a camp there." She seemed unconcerned.

"A camp? I don't understand. Who is with you?" I was confused.

"No one. Should there be? I'm big now. I can be by myself for a while." Her little chin was held high with this.

A remarkably independent and sturdy little soldier, I thought.

"Do you want to play catch? Here!" and she threw the ball at me.

We threw the ball back and forth for a while— she grunting and making little child sounds as she used all her might and energy running back and forth, letting out little exclamations when she made an especially good catch.

"This is the most fun!" she exclaimed in her little animated voice. "I wish you would come every day!"

"Do *you* come here every day?" I asked, curious.

"Oh, yes. Sometimes I feed the birds and the squirrels. They're my friends." She looked at me with deep brown eyes.

"I'm sure they are. But don't you have someone to be with? Surely you have an aunt or a guardian."

"They're not expecting me yet. It's too early. Besides, I don't have any homework. It's Sunday."

"Yes, it's Sunday." I wasn't quite satisfied.

And then, remembering something, "What camp are your parents in?"

"Oh, it's a kind of a holiday camp. I don't know much about it. They've been there since Pearl Beach, I think."

"You mean Pearl Harbor?" I suggested, immediately seizing on the stories and reports I had heard about the internment of thousands of Japanese-American citizens after the attack of December 7, 1941. Amache, Colorado, was one of ten such camps. Good Lord, this was 1945! What was this child doing here by herself? Surely she was with some relatives, or friends of her parents.

"What is your name?" I asked.

"Terumi," she replied.

"That's Japanese, isn't it?" I knew the answer.

"I don't know, but my parents don't talk about it much. They said to tell everyone I was Chinese. But I don't think I'm Chinese, do you?" and she looked up at me with her head cocked to one side, with that innocence that only children and animals can possess.

"No, Terumi, I don't think you're Chinese." There was silence for a few moments.

"Well, anyway, I have to go home now." She unexpectedly took my hand and pulled me toward the gate.

We walked for a few minutes, and then I asked, "Terumi, do you have any relatives, any cousins or brothers or sisters to play with?"

"No one around here. But mother used to talk about my older sister. She was in the war across the ocean. I don't know what happened to her, but they don't talk about her any more. I was too little then anyway—I didn't know her." She spoke casually and without any seeming remorse or sense of loss. She spoke, I noticed, in the past tense.

"I guess she was a musician—a good one," she added.

"What did she play?" I asked, but I already knew.

"The violin," she answered. "I guess she was real good."

"Did she—die?" I asked gently, holding my breath.

"I don't know. Mother and Father just don't talk about her any more. They just don't." And that seemed final.

"How often do you talk with your parents?" I was curious.

"Whenever I want."

"Of course, of course." Yet, I couldn't imagine easy communications with the internment camp.

"What was your sister's—what is her name?"

"I don't know. They just called her 'Sis' and that's all."

She seemed to tire of this subject and started running ahead.

"You know what?" She turned excitedly.

"What?" I asked, amused at her seamless energy.

"When I grow up, I want someone just like you to play with!"

"You need someone your own age," I admonished her.

"Oh, you can never find anyone your own age. They're all gone now anyway."

How true those words rang—"You can never find anyone...."

"All gone?" I thought. What did she mean?

"Surely, you have other little friends." I looked at her grave little face and felt suddenly very sorry for her. No parents, no playmates, no little friends—how alone this tiny child was!

"No. But now I have you."

"But I live very far away, and I must soon leave for home—tomorrow, in fact." I hated to tell her.

"Oh." She looked downcast for a moment, then recovered in a flash. She looked up at me and added excitedly, "Then I'll write to you—I can write real good!"

"Fine, little princess—you will write to me...." and with an afterthought, "and may I write to you in return?"

"Oh, you won't have to. I suppose you're busy. That's all right."

Cheerfully said, but was she being evasive? "Then you *will* write?" I pressed the point.

"Well, yes."

"Then here is my address." I took out a soiled piece of music transcript paper, one with my name and university address stamped on it, tore off a large section, and gave it to her, "I am going to expect a letter very soon." She took it and gazed at the name and address for a while.

Abruptly, she ran over to a nearby bench, picked up an old, weathered knapsack, and placed the paper carefully inside.

"You'll get one. You'll see. Real soon." And she threw the ball at me once more—or almost at me. Once again I had to lurch sideways to catch it, but this time I kept my game hand well-concealed and, subsequently, missed the ball completely.

"It's okay," she encouraged, "you can use your other hand. I don't mind." And she smiled a wise little smile.

"Goodbye, I have to go now." She paused and, frowning, looked up at the sky for a moment, as if checking for something. And then, "Thanks a lot for playing with me." She turned and ran down the path and was gone. I dimly and unconsciously noticed the song of birds return once more.

I wrapped my faithful scarf around my neck walked slowly back to the hotel. I wondered to myself, if I returned tomorrow and waited for her, would Terumi come back to the park to play?

For a long time, after returning to my room, I sat and pondered the question. No answer was forthcoming, and nothing in my capacity to reason or imagine could help answer that perplexing unknown.

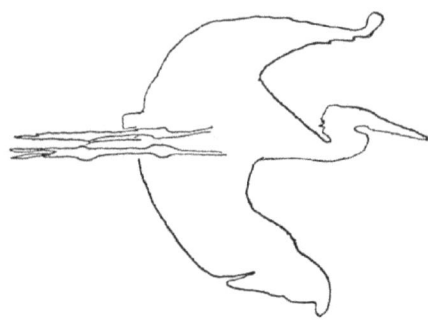

Chapter IX

In a faraway land, somewhere between Eastern Europe and the great Soviet Plains, an aging artist looked about him and pondered the long path ahead. His talents, of some renown, had nonetheless never produced the one piece – that singular moment that would carry his years of practice and study into the repertory of the Great Masters.

He bore his easel and palette, heavy oil paints and French chalk and heavily wrapped brushes and spatulae strapped to his back, as if for an Alpine ascent.

It was a cold, gray, wintry day that the old man trudged quietly up the mountain road. He had left the village far behind in his journey to the grotto by the stream.

Years ago, the old man had found the grotto on one of his solitary sojourns to the woods. He enjoyed being alone and found great solace in the quiet these woods provided. The noise of the village folk grew tiresome to him, and he much preferred the haunting Birdsongs and the tumbling energy of the stream. Only there, he knew, could he find peace and time to think, to look back.

His life had passed quietly by, barely noticed by his neighbors. He went about his simple chores each day, preferring privacy to companionship. He knew no one with whom he could speak or live in comfort.

For many years, he went his way, bothering no one, sometimes rebuking a friendly hand with a gruffness he would always regret, but could not help. On church days, he would come late, stand unseen in the shadows of the foyer, and worship quietly. His faith, indeed, in whatever Power there might be behind that altar, was his only tie with his fellow villagers.

And as the seasons metamorphosed from warm to chill, from cold to spring, his hair grew slowly white, his hands became course and rough, and his beard more craggy. Yet his brittle blue eyes remained sharp and bright, even as his body became more bent. Like an aging oak, he stooped to meet the ground, and only a sturdy cane of elm allowed him to take his long walks. Still, though his once brisk and forceful stride had become a shuffle, he never failed to visit his friendly woods on special days.

This day was that one special time of the year when the old man took his longest and most strenuous walk. The villagers were busy preparing for their Christmas merrymaking, a time when the old man felt especially uncomfortable. He never took part in the festivities and he became even more quarrelsome than usual. His journey took him many miles above the village, far beyond where picnickers go, to the snow and pine trees – and to the grotto by the stream. As he struggled slowly up the path, blowing warm mist into the cold December air, his memories took him back to those days long past when, as a child, he ran and skipped and played with his small friends. Cold air stung his ice-blue eyes as he remembered running through the snow, back to that warm cottage of another land. A crackling hearth and the aroma of strange and wonderful creations from the kitchen became as real as the snow that chilled him now.

A young girl appeared in his memory, and her laughing face and mist-shining hair bore heavily on his consciousness. She danced and sang and smiled at him – she took his hand and drew him out and pirouetted around his bewildered, bemused figure. Flowers filled the air with a long-forgotten fragrance. Then, just as suddenly as the presentiment had appeared, it began to fade, and the laughing girl became indistinct, translucent, then wispy and ghostlike. She beckoned to him, sadly now, then became a vaporous, fading spectre, and was gone.

Hours later, as the old man turned the last bend in the old abandoned pathway, he was greatly surprised to come upon a man sitting on a large stone. Disgruntled by this interruption in his isolation and reverie, the old man tried to walk past unnoticed, for he could see that the man's head was cast down and supported by his hands and arms on his knees. But before he could slip by, the second man looked up suddenly and said, "Hello, old man. Delay a moment if you will." His voice was raspy and weak.

Surprised, and still put off by this intrusion, the old man replied, "What is it that causes you to bid me so? And what are you doing in these abandoned woods?"

"I beseech your help, old man," the younger one replied. And the old man could see now the scruffy face of an unkempt, thirty-year old traveler, obviously weary from his laborious climb.

"And what help could an old and stooping soul as I be to you, so much younger, and thus stronger?" Yet, he could see that this man was weakened and in poor repair.

"As you can see, I am not as strong as my years would will, and I have been...I have, unfortunately, a game leg." With this, he struggled to his feet, revealing what appeared to be a ragged, torn and soiled coat, of a color strange, yet hauntingly familiar. Beneath this full-length and tattered habiliment, the old man could just make out what appeared to be the remains of an old and dated uniform. The exhausted man lurched forward, and the old man grabbed his arm to keep him from falling.

The one gazed at the other, each searching the other's somehow familiar face. "I, too, require a cane," said the younger after a moment, and he limped and tripped around clumsily until he had found his cane beneath some wet leaves and snow. "Will you help me to the grotto, old man?" he asked, supporting himself on the cane and on the old man's sturdy arm.

"The grotto? The grotto?" repeated the old man, with disappointment in his voice. "You know of the grotto?"

"Yes, I have heard of the grotto by the stream. I must see it before I...go."

"But this is a place most private, indeed sacred, to me!" cried the old man.

He had felt an ominous sense of finality as he left the village that morning. His bones were warning him of something, and he was afraid to focus for long on that warning. Certainly, he resented the appearance of this interloper, now of all times!

"Yet, I beseech your help. I will be quiet and discreet. I will leave you to your thoughts and your privacy. If only I might see the grotto!" The old man could not refuse the cripple's plea, and he reluctantly held out his arm as the two struggled up the hill together.

As the two weary travelers limped and pulled themselves around to the last turn in the road, the grotto appeared. Mist swirled around an eruption of stone on the far side of an idyllic, glassy pond. The stream which raced noisily into the upside of the pond became instantly silent as it filled the basin of the grotto. Green and black in color, the pond moved silently to the right where it erupted once again into a relentless cataract.

"At last!" exclaimed the younger man. "I have seen the grotto! And it is even more remarkable than the pictures in my mind! No wonder, old man, you want no interruption or intrusion on your time spent here."

"Indeed!" replied the elder, "So respect my age and wishes, and leave me to my interlude." But before the young man could turn, the rustling of leaves behind them caused them both to whirl about.

There, holding a broken bough, stood a forlorn creature, a girl of perhaps twenty years. The coat she wore was old, as if handed down from mother to child, to child, to child. Her hands were cold and white, her shoes badly worn and in tatters. Poor protection, thought the two, against these unforgiving elements.

"And who are *you*?" exploded the old man. "How came you by this isolated sanctuary?"

"I am lost, old man," replied the young girl, obviously cold and frightened. "May I join you for company and protection? I fear I have wandered too far and have lost my way." With this, the girl approached closer and the old man noticed that she was unusually homely, so unattractive that he was somewhat revulsed. He could not say what part of her face was the source of this revulsion, but whether it was the malformed and scarred nose, the vapid, colorless eyes, or the small, tight mouth, he nevertheless averted his eyes. Her pleading eyes could not be avoided, but certainly he did not have to look long at the deformed and potted skin!

"I will be busy here for some time. Perhaps you and my fellow traveler here will be able to occupy yourselves and leave me to myself until I call for you." And before they could answer, he turned stiffly about, and shuffled and stomped erratically toward the grotto.

The old man sat for some time, gazing at the tall accumulation of stone and rock across the pond. Memories of youth and friends again coursed through his mind. School days blended gradually into more remote and darker shadows. The flash of thunder and lightning on distant shores drew a sharp breath from his throat – the crack and clang of giant machines, the terrible explosions, the thudding of dark, falling bodies caused him to stir uncomfortably. The cacophony of some distant discord deafened him. Then – silence. And a delicate mist hung ghostlike over a marsh in a faraway field. Broken musketry jutted up in grotesquely reminiscent forms. And only silence....

As the old man wandered through is memories, he was made conscious of some movement to his left. Something was floating toward him on the pond. He turned his head to see a small green ball bobbing toward him. For reasons he did not understand, he reached out, and as the errant toy swept by, he seized it. It was a scruffy ball, some sort of soft material. The old man turned it around in his hand, wondering from whence upstream it had come. It appeared very old on more careful scrutiny. Several areas were stained and flat. And some small pieces of its surface had long ago been lost.

"A curious thing," mused the old man to himself. "Older than a house, yet what started it on this present journey?" As he was wondering to himself, a call from nearby came to him.

"Old man, what have you there?" The younger man, still looking haggard and worn, came toward him.

"Is it a ball?" asked the homely girl. "Yes, a green ball," she answered her own question. "Where did you come upon it, old man?"

"It came upon *me!*" stated the old man gruffly. "Another unwanted interruption." And he started to throw it back into the pond.

"Wait!" cried the girl, "Please don't throw it away. I would like it!"

"Why would anyone want such a wasted artifact?" demanded the old man. "It has no worth and certainly no use!"

"It might have some use. Please, may I have it?"

She was so animated and persistent that the old man begrudgingly turned himself stiffly around and threw the ball toward her. He had expected a painful response to his efforts, remembering his stiffened joints and aging muscles.

But there was no pain.

The ball sailed through the air, farther than he thought he had thrown it. And the young girl leapt high in the air to catch it, her torn and tattered clothes whipping around her bony legs.

She caught it with one hand high above her head – a remarkable feat! She laughed a loud and echoing laugh, and turned to the young cripple some yards away.

"Your turn, my soldier! Catch!" And she hurled the ball as hard as she could. It sailed above the younger man's head. He twisted to catch it and his cane flew from his hand. The old man, standing by now started for a moment, expecting him to fall.

Instead, the long coat of the soldier sailed in full circle, and he gracefully leapt sideways, then back, then up to intercept the little green missile.

"Back to you, old man!" And before the elder could object, he saw the speck of green flying toward him. But to his amazement, the ball began to float, then to dart about, as if it had its own life. It flashed past the old man's outstretched hands and onto the rocks behind him. It bounced and skittered from rock to rock, evading the old man as he skipped skillfully behind it, reaching out now, dodging sideways then, jumping from this rock to that.

And as the three chased the mischievous green ball, their laughing efforts took on the form of a graceful ballet seen in slow motion, A pas de trois among three weightless and ephemeral specters.

The soldier was once again whole, no limp to be seen, his sturdy limbs hurling him aloft in effortless coordination.

The girl was glowing, radiant, beautiful, her tattered garb transformed into sparkling folds of gold.

The old man was old no more. His crooked spine was straight, his gnarled hands now smooth and strong. He laughed as he danced and jumped across the stones, all pain and stiffness gone.

And the green ball soared up and down, now bouncing here, now rolling there. And the Birdsong became more rich and vibrant, in perfect harmony with this Dance of Joy.

And laughter and grace and strength and beauty filled the grotto that day.

The old man chased the ball down past a large and overhanging aspen grove, leafless and thick of limb. He could hear the laughter of the strong young soldier and the beautiful young girl fading behind him. He looked and looked but could not find the ball. No turning of rocks or sweeping away of branches revealed the little lost toy.

He returned finally, disappointed and weary from the search.

As he came back to the grotto, he stopped abruptly and looked desperately around. There was silence. The two were not to be seen. The laughter had disappeared. No evidence of the ballet was to be seen anywhere.

The Birdsong had ceased.

The old man looked and called out for a long time. No answer was forthcoming. Nothing of the soldier or the girl could be found. And now it was darkening in the woods.

He finally sat down heavily by his pond and gazed across at the grotto. His breath began to come more heavily and his bones began to ache. He tried to reach for his old cane, but his twisted and gnarled hand could not quite grasp it. He knew he could not get up without it.

Exhausted, he leaned back against the tree and closed his eyes. Snow began to fall lightly. It was getting darker. The Birdsong did not return.

"I'll sleep for a moment now," he thought. "Then I'll look for my friends. Perhaps they will help me find the little green ball." He smiled at the thought. And he fell into a deep, deep, sleep...

When the leaves that covered him were finally brushed away, there was found beside his rigid form a half-buried canvas which, when extricated, revealed a vibrant image of unforgettable beauty and radiance, frozen, even as its author, forever in time.

Many years later when it was finally displayed in the Great Museum of St. Petersburg, no one who gazed upon it could ever dismiss the haunting imagery of an old and bent voyager, gazing intently and with obvious fascination toward the athletic form of a young warrior stretched forward from the throw. Past him, to the ephemeral beauty of that exquisite young palaestrian, extended forever upward, her lovely Asian countenance looking heavenward past a glowing sphere clutched above her, emanating timeless life through her fingers – the green ball.

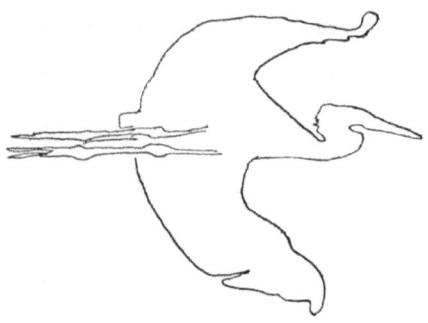

Chapter X

I didn't see Sadako all that summer, but I thought of her often. I missed her lilting voice and hooded, twinkling brown eyes. We had spent essentially no real time together, and despite the long wait, she did not appear. The summer shadows began to grow longer. September arrived with its somber forebodings of the chill to come. Indian summer brought with it those early subtle changes in the air, those forewarnings of the end of the glorious Elysian months and the beginning of autumn.

Work on the sonata was progressing fairly well, though the second movement, the adagio, lay incomplete on the piano.

"I must find some deeper urge, some inspiration to complete this work," I said to myself one day.

But where to go? I tried listening to recordings of the great sonatas and quartets of Beethoven and Bartòk (Ives' were not yet recorded), but I feared greatly being overly influenced by those enormous works. Further, neither man had concentrated nearly as much on the lyrical mood as I intended for my composition.

Walking through Chicago's parks was singularly ineffective in producing any artistic stimulus whatsoever. Indeed, Chicago was beginning to have a deadly and negative effect on my creative impulse, and I longed for some gentler fields, some older, distant paths to walk and ponder.

New England was the natural solution to this need. I knew from past journeys that nowhere else could I find that particular blend of tree and fence, of form and mood. Only the lovely, lonely back roads of Vermont and New Hampshire could bring me the special ambience I needed now.

I knew that I must go and shortly made plans. Leon would take care of my class the last week in September, and his associate would cover for me the first week in October. My old '37 Dodge would be just fine, as long as the heater worked and it didn't rain too much.

I departed one brisk early morning, the sharp misty air lying fog-like over the autumn grass. My heart seemed filled with hope and expectation, as if some grand promise was soon to be fulfilled.

Driving alone was quite pleasant, and when I couldn't find music on the scratchy old radio I hummed aloud. Of course, I was not really alone, for Princess, my kitten-friend, sat like a royal passenger on a pillow I had brought just for her.

She was a good traveler, and kept me good company. A warm, furry, silken friend to pet when the roads were straight, and to laugh at when she was tossed about on the winding parts

We made good time, and in two days, we had passed through New York and had entered Vermont.

It was our good luck that an early frost had been there before us, for the foliage had begun to change. Misty morning dampness slowly gave way to the irrepressible sun, and each golden ray illuminated another cluster of flowering dogwood, another grove of delicate elms, a patch of yellow mustard. Wild cherry and geraniums shone for the last time that year and the marigold were already starting to fade. White pine mingled with luminous maple trees, and marsh blue violets lent somber contrast to their florid exuberance.

We drove southeast on Highway 22A from Charlotte, through Vergennes toward Middlebury.

We saw the old polygonal barn at Ferrisburg designed in 1911, and we walked along Buckwheat Street, past the old cemetery.

I thought of Rokeby, Ferrisburg, home of Rowland E. Robinson, Vermont's reclusive 19th century illustrator and writer. Folklore was his forte, and locals still talk about his stories, his extended hikes into the back forest, burdened by snowshoes and musket, his long white beard shining with morning dew.

I walked among the grand old buildings at Middlebury College, inhaling the peculiar yet familiar aroma of freshly mowed grass mingled with cedar smoke curling from the faculty home chimneys.

Each stop brought a different visual and sensual message, and renewed the treasured but buried memories of time spent foraging these same back roads. It seemed that crusty, sturdy old New England filled a special and distinct void that no other experience could. And it never changed.

I was musing to myself, as I strolled comfortably down one of the older, oak-lined streets in Middlebury, when I saw her. She was sitting under an old elm tree, back on the grass, preoccupied with some flowers she held.

There could be no doubt—and as she responded to my cry of surprise, Sadako turned and said, "Professor Danbury, you've come to Middlebury!" and her sad eyes showed surprise.

"Is *this* where you attend school? No wonder I've never been able to find you!"

"I spend some time here. It is very beautiful—and—peaceful. One has time to rest and think." She looked tired and more pale than I had remembered, and much more mature. I recalled her pallid face at Christmas, but then I had imagined that the artificial lights had cast that white and cold glare upon her face. Now, on closer scrutiny, she appeared more frail and delicate than I had remembered her, and her lips had lost that rubric vitality that they had shown before. And I noticed that the wound on her hand, though turned away from me, had not healed.

"Are you well, Sadako?" I did not try to hide my concern.

"Yes, Professor. As well as I could be." She pronounced this solemnly.

"But you do not look well; you are pale and—I believe you've lost some weight." I was truly concerned.

"My diet is not the best," she smiled gently. "And my studies are rigorous and demanding."

"The violin—are you practicing?"

"Perhaps too much." She looked off at something dreamily. "But it is worth it." She looked suddenly at me and smiled warmly. "You will be very proud."

"I know I will be—what are you working on?"

"The Bartòk and Beethoven—the ones you love."

A little disappointed, I asked, "And?"

"And...and other works—modern works—you will be very pleased when you hear them. And," looking down, "who is this?"

Her voice turned up and, for a moment, a spark of the old life flickered across her face.

Princess had hopped from under the small blanket I always carried while strolling. She ran immediately to Sadako and jumped into her lap.

"What a lovely little friend you have! My, isn't she special?" And she held the kitten aloft, all limp and purring. "What is her name?"

"Princess," I replied, leaving the previous conversation for another time.

"Princess! Of course—Princess Aki!" Sadako snuggled the kitten to her face, and it seemed for a brief moment that a sudden surge of life passed from that tiny, warm animal to the cold and delicate creature holding her.

"Sadako," I said, "do you have some time to yourself this week?"

"Well," after thinking a moment, "today is Thursday. After class tomorrow, I have nothing but my practice until Monday." She looked up at me, "Why?"

"Well," I hesitated. "I'm driving on to New Hampshire and could use somewhat more company than Princess can afford. What do you think of joining me?" I held my breath.

"Oh, Professor! I would love to join you! I must—I would love to spend that time with you!" She seemed elated; in fact, she seemed to be as relieved as I.

"Wonderful! It's settled then. I'll pick you up tomorrow, at...?"

"Four o'clock."

"Where? At your residence?" But I anticipated her reply.

"Out by the wishing well—you passed it on the way in." She seemed so much more animated and alive now.

"Yes, I know it. Tomorrow, then." And I reached out my hands to help her up, forgetting for a moment....She grasped both hands firmly and stood up, holding on tightly as she stood looking at me. I tried to free my poor, crippled hand from her grasp, but she was tenacious and would not let go.

"I am so glad you came, Charles!"

Finally, relaxing and suppressing my eternal self-directed revulsion, "As am I, Sadako." I felt caught in that time warp that seemed always to surround her. An aura of calm and eternal peace seemed to encompass us. Then she turned and walked quickly up the path.

I did not notice for some time that I was standing alone. The sun had passed behind some clouds and the pressure of little Princess against my leg finally roused me.

"In the winter in the woods alone
against the trees I go."
Robert Frost
"In The Clearing"

111

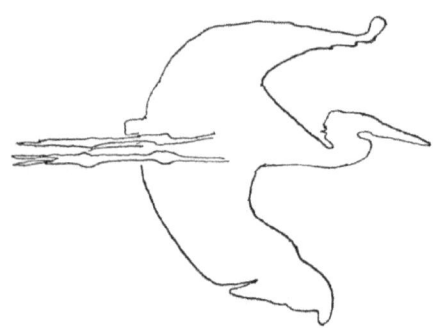

Chapter XI

We were all bundled up, blankets around our knees, the old Dodge purring along with Princess contented on Sadako's lap.

"I know a place, Charles." Sadako said quietly. She held firmly onto my arm with her mittened hand.

"Where, Sadako?"

"It is north of here. Not too far. It is beautiful." She seemed more frail today— or was I imagining it?

"Tell me about it."

"If you turn north on Highway 14, there's a lovely area where two ponds lie close together. I have been there once, long ago," She stared dreamily out the windshield.

"Do you want to go there, Sadako?" I asked gently.

"Yes, Charles." She spoke with quiet conviction. "This once more."

"Of course." Her words disturbed me.

We drove essentially alone up Route 14, no traffic on that Friday to distract us. As we passed East Montpelier, the autumnal glow cast its blush of golds, yellows, oranges and reds so brilliantly that the colors literally reflected off the shiny asphalt road.

I could pick out old friends from childhood days, happy days, when we had named our favorite trees. There was the Butterscotch Tree and the Marmalade Tree, the Fire Engine Tree and the Rainbow Tree. I saw the Old Rusty Tree and the Raspberry Tree and the Plum Jam tree. None had changed—they were exactly as I remembered them—not a leaf out of place!

There is a richness and intensity of tones, a gay riot of extravagant hues found only in that northeast corner of this land. And no matter how often one returns to greet that chromatic spectrum, he will be richly rewarded each time, and the shock of recognition can never be diluted or diminished.

Yet, an unfamiliar chill was in the air, and for some reason I felt an urgency to move on, an uneasy foreboding of something I could not predict or even focus upon. A strange verse kept recurring in my mind and I could not push it aside   How did it go....?

Deep in my heart a chilling freeze
    Presages Winter's blow.
    What Dionysian fields are these?
    What meadows deep with snow?

Didst Innocents go hand in hand
    And sit beneath that tree?
    Then why wouldst leave this
    rainbow'd land, to search on endlessly?

Behold these woodlands where we talked
    Of Autumn's radiant glow,
    Those joyous byways where we walked,
    But can no longer go.

Three miles north of Kent's Corner we followed the signs to North Calais, then veered left for approximately a half-mile more.

Suddenly, spectacularly, shimmering as would a jeweled reflecting glass, Mirror Lake appeared.

Sadako held my arm tightly.

"Remarkable!" I exclaimed. "Exquisite! No wonder you wanted to return." I pulled over along the road and drove slowly down to the lake's edge.

We sat there for several minutes, gazing out over the glassy sheet of ebony green water. No other travelers were to be seen, and as we sat there in silence, the eerie cry of the loon came hauntingly across that pond.

"A sound of a distant horn
O'er shadowed lake is borne...""
C.E. Ives, 1906

"There is more," Sadako said in hushed tones, afraid to spoil the moment.

"Impossible," I said quietly.

"Yes, Charles. If you drive a little further up the road, you will see."

I restarted the engine and drove slowly up the dirt road. After a few hundred yards, we emerged from a thick cluster of trees, and there, under a misty blanket, lay Nelson Pond. As Mirror Lake was spectacular, Nelson Pond was uncannily serene, the peculiar arrangement of estuaries and inlets, contrasted against thorny fingers of tree-covered promontories, creating a supernal scene. A thin, wispy shroud of low-lying mist added an ethereal pall over the entire vision. And a delicate, fragrant effluence emanated from the russet meadow beyond.

We had arrived at the very wellspring I had sought. Here, indeed, was inspiration!

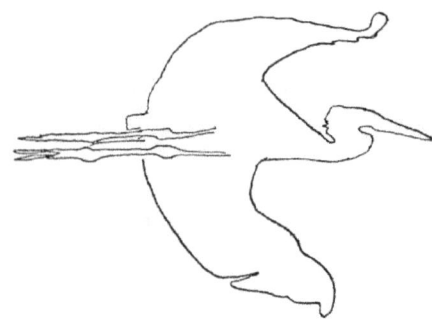

Chapter XII

For many hours we sat on the grassy edge, gazing dreamily out over the motionless pond. We talked of the past and the present, but avoided mention of tomorrow. We spoke of our first meeting in Chicago, of Christmas lights, of humid hot Chicago summers, of violins.

While we talked, a brown and red butterfly flitted past me and alighted on a pink clover next to Sadako. She gently brushed its wings with the back of her fingers. It flattened out momentarily, then rose erratically up, circled us several times, then struck out across the pond.

"Look, Charles," said Sadako. "How delicate and fragile it is! How could anyone destroy it?"

"What do you mean, 'destroy'?" I asked.

"Some pin it to a paper as a specimen. Its life is so brief—so ephemeral anyway, why shorten it? Must men always destroy beauty?"

"I'm afraid it is his nature, Sadako. And the most fragile and helpless always seem to suffer first and suffer most. The butterfly's freedom and innocence are no protection."

After a long pause, during which Sadako and Princess played with an acorn, Sadako turned to me and said, "Charles?" She looked frail and lovely, her black hair and pale skin complementing the same hues in the kitten's coat. "Have you finished the adagio?"

"Yes, I have."

"I knew you would. It was only a matter of time."

"But it had to be now, didn't it?" I asked, looking at her with quiet interest.

"What do you mean?" She seemed puzzled—or did she?

"I think you know. Would you share the thoughts that crossed your mind a while back?"

"What thoughts?" She seemed slightly uneasy.

"Sadako, while we were talking a while ago, I mentioned how terrible the August heat was in Chicago this year."

"Yes?"

"You became very uneasy at that point, and tried to change the subject. Why?"

"I—I don't know, Charles." She seemed suddenly frightened.

"Sadako, think a moment. Something about August or Chicago struck a chord somewhere inside you, as it is doing so now. Look at you! You're trembling. What could it be, Sadako? What is frightening you so?!"

But no more was spoken. Sadako moved closer to me, rested her head on my shoulder and held tightly onto my arm. Soon, the sun had set, and the cold air began to creep around us.

Sadako stirred. High above, a wedge of geese was flying southward against the hard October chill, and their desolate honking had aroused her. Then her eyes widened.

"Sembazuru! – Chizuru!" she exclaimed.

"What?" I asked.

"Cranes," she said, suddenly sitting up.

"No, my dear. Geese. Snow geese flying south for the winter."

"Cranes!" she repeated. "A thousand cranes!" and she started to cry quietly. "I am so afraid. It is too soon, yet so late."

"What do you mean, 'too soon?' Sadako, what is it?"

"I don't know. There is a terrible storm coming. It is growing closer. I can feel its presence everywhere. I see a great, boiling sea. Everywhere, there are eyes—horrified eyes! Some are burning!! Hot wind is tearing at the trees—the buildings, the people! And, oh! The children!! The poor little children—screaming and running—looking for mothers! But, I see no mothers—only smoking, smoldering piles of clothing—melting with the burning ground. Oh, God, it is so horrible, so desolate—so *final*!" She was profoundly frightened, and looked at me with the frightened eyes of a fawn petrified in the imminent presence of a great and deadly panther.

"Sadako, what is this great fear? If it had form and substance, I would surely rid you of it if I could."

The geese passed by, and slowly, Sadako recovered and began to relax somewhat; she eventually fell into a fitful sleep.

Later, we drove home in silence, she with her head on my shoulder, her arm wrapped in mine. And little Princess cuddled and purred on Sadako's lap, lending what solace she could to these two troubled friends.

And there is at times a
bleakness...which settles
down grimly...over the broken
hills."
                                Thoreau

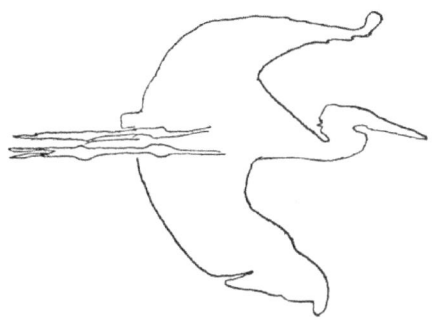

Chapter XIII

After leaving Sadako at Middlebury the next morning, I did not plan to see her again for a while, for she could not tell me where she could be reached. She promised to contact me before the performance of the sonata, which was scheduled to take place in December. I was not satisfied, but accepted her promise.

For the next two months, I labored without rest over the rehearsals. I had finally solved the vexing enigma of the adagio. Instead of the solo violin playing the principal theme, which seemed too grand, too overwhelming for one instrument, I provided *two* violins to struggle with its complexities. It would break precedence, but wouldn't Ives have laughed at the objection? Then, from the second to the final movement, the allegro molto, I let *two* voices sing with all the power that those twin instruments could hurl against the orchestra. A convoluted fugal progression diatonically expanding from restrained and haunting beauty to a turbulent, frenzied storm of polytonal explosions—a violent finale!

It was thus decided, and the work came easily. Soon it was ready for first rehearsal. John Mallory played first violin and his finest student, Lorie Dinetti, would take the second part. All went well, and even the older professionals were moved by the results.

But I could not deny the sense of loss I felt during the post-rehearsal critiques. As the musicians buzzed about, working with Leon who was conducting, I was distracted by my thoughts of Sadako.

A curious and somber mood passed over me at times, like a great gray bird casting its shadow. During those short moments, there came the cold and chilling apparition of a desolate, frozen marsh—devoid of all life. And always overhead, a great thundercloud hovering ominously over the

land. The only sound to be heard was the haunting cry of the loon.

These short dreams would pass quickly, but I
was always left with a sense of foreboding—and of
great loss and sadness.

The evening of the concert had arrived. I left
Princess alone at the apartment, some food and
milk arranged for her. She thumped happily to the
door to see me off, her little bell tinkling away as
she went.

Curious, I thought. I had almost forgotten the
little bell that Sadako had bought for Princess in
the small Grafton Village Store in Vermont. I remembered Sadako tying the little toy around
Princess' neck and saying, "There, little Princess
Suzuko—little Princess of the Bells. You cannot
forget me now. Nor can your father, for every
time you run and play, he'll have to think of me—
and there's nothing he can do about it." And she
laughed that lilting laugh in harmony with the
tinkling bell.

As I arrived at the concert hall, I noticed a brisk snowfall just starting—yet the air was not chilly or biting.

As I was entering the auditorium through the side door to meet Leon, I noticed some steam coming from a basement window.

"Hello, Charles, my good friend." He grasped my hand and shook it enthusiastically. "Great news, Charles! Frachelli is in the audience. Word of your sonata has leaked out, and I hear he's interested in performing it."

"Frachelli?? Well, good for us—we finally rate a first-class review." And then, "Say, Leon, I noticed some steam coming from the basement—any problems?"

"I don't think so. Apparently the furnace is acting up a bit and the engineer is down there fussing with it. Don't worry, it'll be taken care of."

"Okay" I said. Yet something in the back of my mind began to stir.

The first movement went well, and from my vantage point behind the curtains, I could see Frachelli in the front row, leaning forward, listening intensely with a curious half-smile on his face.

As the second movement began, with the long, arching lyrical cadenza by the first violin, I thought I could smell more than the musty steam. A more acrid aroma seemed to come from behind me, and I glanced around. No smoke. The back-stage manager's assistant got up and disappeared through a back door.

I studied Frachelli's granite features as the second violinist stood up and joined with Mallory. Together, they began the duet that was to make the work famous. The two hurled their song to the heavens as the orchestra surged behind them. I could see Frachelli's eyes glistening as the culminating point of that monstrous theme, that searing rhapsodic elegy, soared heavenward.

And the adagio flowed into the allegro without the customary interruption, a seamless transgression against unwritten rules, against academic prejudice that said it couldn't, it mustn't be done.

But there it was, the dueling orchestra and two violins bursting headlong into the final movement, without a pause for protocol.

Frachelli was sitting upright—a huge man, with great powerful hands on his knees—enthralled by the sound. He was transfixed, and I will not forget the expression on his face.

But coincidental with the last scherzo, smoke began to seep through the floors. Almost immediately I heard a murmur from the first few rows, and I could see animated figures pointing at the stage from out of the darkness of the audience. Someone screamed as a belch of gray smoke burst from behind the brass section.

Most of the orchestra, facing forward, could not see the smoke and had continued playing.

Suddenly, there was an explosion of such intensity that I was thrown against a wall and momentarily struck unconscious. As I came to, great confusion confronted me. The hall was filled with smoke and flames, and people and musicians were running in all directions. A choking cloud fell over everyone, and some were lying between rows of seats struggling for breath.

I was trying to free myself from between two fallen beams when, above the melee, suddenly I heard it—unreal, impossibly clear, just as I had heard it that cold day outside the Performing Arts Building. I twisted painfully and could see someone leading Frachelli toward an exit—yet he turned back and faced the stage transfixed. It was apparent through the clouds of smoke that he, too, heard that sound—the soaring glory of the virtuoso *solo* violin caught in a moment of transcendental creation.

Then I saw him caught up by the panicking throng, and he disappeared, being dragged roughly through the door. I felt someone or something tug at me violently and push me toward the backstage door. Other hands grabbed at me and pulled me into the cold, clear air outside, but I caught one last glance at the inferno within. With horror, I saw—I know I saw—that pallid face, those sad brown eyes, a torn and smoking schoolgirl frock. She seemed to reach out once more with scalded hand—not for help, but as if to say goodbye.

Then, reverting to another stage—a classic tongue—she says,

"Addio, Charles, Addio.
"Good-bye, Charles, good-bye.

Il mare, il porto—tutto e finito.
The sea, the port—all is finished.
Ah, non piangere.
Ah, don't cry.

A te I rai degli astir d'or...
On you shine the rays of the
golden star...

Mio name é non Dolore—ma Gioia!!"
My name is not Sorrow—but
   Joy!!"

She looks up past the billowing smoke—

Ride il ciel—
"The sky is smiling—
Ah, serrena notte—quanta stella!"
Ah, clear night—so many stars!"

And then, turning to Charles—

"It is done, Charles. We are resurrected from a common Fire. To his own Destiny each now must go.
Farewell!!"

She turns to face what was the auditorium, and with a sad, luminescent smile, says,

"Ah, dolce Morta—Son qui!
"Now, sweet Death—I am here!

Sono finito!—Vien!"
I have finished!—Come!"

And before I could move, she seemed to become translucent, a ghostly wisp, losing form and acuity, slowly becoming indistinct, then suddenly disappearing behind an impenetrable wall of flames and crashing girders and concrete.

A dungeon horrible, on all sides
  round,
As one great furnace flowed; yet
  from those flames
No (visible) light, but rather darkness
  bound.
  Milton
  Paradise Lost, Book I

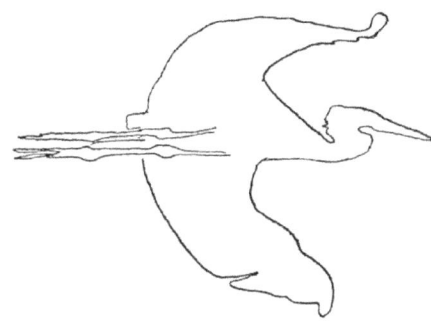

Chapter XIV

In a darkening glen, a small girl sets aside her toy ball and stands upright, frail and alone. Her ragged little gray-white knee socks are old and frayed. Her blue skirt and white blouse are dusty and aging. The ribbon of her straw hat is torn. The gay woven butterfly of her lapel has faded.

She gazes past a towering gray slab jutting starkly into the skies, grotesquely out of place in this silent wood. Little Terumi, née Kazuko, née Aiko, looks past that somber stone, up to the firmaments. She does not notice, nor can she read, the strange language or the 101,693 names etched into that colossal monolith.

As her eyes fix on the cosmic hyaline beyond and upon the emerging stars, she shivers for a moment. Then, aloud, she begins to recite:

"Please, Death, hold back,
For yet a little while—"

The only sound is the hissing of the wind as it turns the tall, brown, parched grass into a ghostly sea. There are no birdsongs. The strident insect chorus has ceased. The flowers stand lifeless—dry and brittle—their petals powdery white, their skeletons blown about and scattered by the merciless wind.

Little Terumi's skin is mottled and covered with violaceous, weeping sores that will not heal. She is dying from the same Malignant Isolation that has decimated all of her Brothers and Sisters, her Mothers and her Fathers.

As the dark, dispassionate heavens absorb all sound and light, all color and movement from the Earth, leaving it a barren, orbiting Shrine, Terumi waits patiently in endless, timeless pain—a tiny, pitiful, voiceless Saint who must ultimately ascend, untethered, forever pure and unblemished, away from the anguished Earth.

I've traveled over rolling sea,
How I came, a mystery.
My ship was launched from
    burning shore.
Banished thenceforth evermore.
I could not sail back 'cross Your
    sea,
Until I turned to gaze on Thee.
Yes, finally knelt and gazed on
    Thee!

136

Addendum

Many years later, when the winter chill was early on the land and the distant rumble of the great city filled the misty air, the graying professor was drawn back to the old Eastern trails, to find, he knew not what.

He made his solitary way along the hard and silent paths to those two lakes. The dry leaves and dead branches crunched and snapped beneath his boots. The familiar, endless brook had not paused, and would not.

But the rainbow leaves were gone; only brown and spiritless skeletons remained, stark and barren, victims of the wind which had stripped them of their colorful habiliments. No gold was left. No orange or red. No yellow crowns or chartreuse cloaks.

All was gone, save the frozen earth and the naked trees. Somber reminders of another time, of a brief moment of light and peace—a stillborn interlude between the sweet and poignant Past and the dim and formless Future.

No little Princess skittered around his heavy boots—no tinkling bells. At each familiar turn he looked for her expectantly, but she did not appear.

Yet the ponds remained unaltered, dark and melancholy—forever fixed in Time and Place—never changing—neither more nor less transcendent in their placid role—To Be.

And the loon's lonely cry could still be heard, floating across the forest floor, echoing from the clear black water through the reaching branches above. Charles sat and listened, and watched, and thought.

Suddenly, the butterfly appeared—a ghostly ballerina pirouetting across the pond, indistinct and tiny—an errant traveler in a forbidding, frozen moment in which she was not meant to be. *Summer* was her domain—yet there she was, struggling against the numbing frost.

Perhaps she had never left.

Now, with her Titian-gilded wings flashing erratically, all movement and energy—across the pond she came.

He watched her stuttering progress and remained motionless—immobilized and strangely rooted in haunting memories, more tree than man.

Then, lo, the tiny thing turned abruptly toward him, circled cautiously, once, twice, three times—then alighted upon his withered, upheld hand. She fluttered there for a moment.

And there in waning sun they stood—he, cast in aging stone; she—poised and vibrant, perched high above on his gnarled, outstretched, lifeless hand—the embodiment of Nature's Promethean flame—an exquisitely winged blossom, the flowering extension and reincarnation of a spent and weary soul.

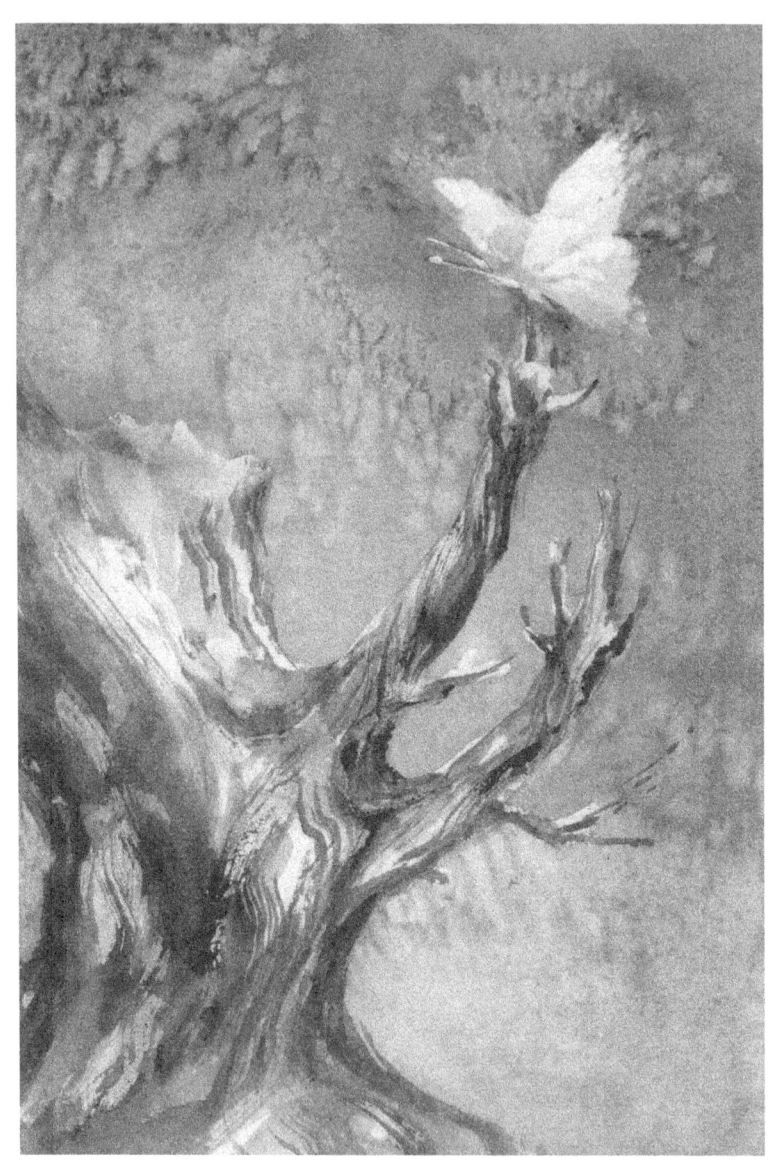

140

Epilogue

From selected notes of C.E. Danbury:

Sometime around Christmas of 1948, I was paging through some old appointment books, which also functioned as diaries, my habit being to jot down important events as they happened.

As I paged through the summer of 1945, that most fateful year of memories, I spied two dates:

August 6, 1945 - bomb dropped on Hiroshima

August 9, 1945 - bomb dropped on Nagasaki

"It was not until many years later, long after my sonata had become part of the world repertory, that I came upon a short article in a national magazine—a small human-interest piece. It read:

Today, ten years after the great bomb exploded over Hiroshima, a young girl name Sadako died of leukemia, one of the complications of exposure to massive doses of radiation. She was two years old when the bomb was dropped.

When her classmates heard that Sadako was ill, they immediately began helping her fold paper sheets into Origami Cranes. In Japan, tradition says that if one folds one thousand Origami

Cranes, their wish is granted. Little Sadako died before they could complete the task.

Exalted Life, predestined Death,
From fertile egg to final breath.
I came from out that sea of Time,
But must return to clay and lime.
If here I now return to die,
Then share, oh friends, my final cry.

And finally, a yellowing letter, folded unevenly fell from a soiled foreign envelope.

I opened the letter carefully and read aloud to myself.

Dear Professor Danbury,

Thank you for stopping to play with me. I am back with my family now. And "Sis" is here too. She says "hello."

You won't have to write—we'll understand.

Terumi

Approximately ninety years ago, between 1904 and 1906, another drama between East and West was taking form. Giacomo Puccini's *Madama Butterfly* had its origins and first performance in Nagasaki, Japan.

144

Glossary

AIKO = Love

AKEMI = Dawn; Morning

AKI = Autumn

CHIZURU = Thousand Cranes

KAZUKO = Child of Peace

SADAKO = Faithful Child

SEMBAZURU = Thousand Cranes

SUZUKO = Small, Round Bells

TERUMI - Luminescence; Beauty

TSURUKO – Crane

Author's Postscript

On Sunday, the 5th of October 1997, I was taking my vacation in New England. As usual, the October colors were gorgeous, and I had deliberately planned my itinerary so that I could follow closely the journey taken by Professor Danbury and Sadako in this book. I had the back windows open for ventilation, and as I came upon the area between Mirror Lake and Nelson Pond (as gorgeous as remembered), suddenly a beautiful white butterfly flew through the open window into the back of the car. She struggled to escape but could not. I stopped the car and watched her erratic flutterings and was reminded instantly of that chapter in "Chizuru" where Danbury and Sadako were sitting at Nelson Pond when the butterfly struggled across to them.

Remarkably, during this interlude, two pieces of music played from the car stereo: one, Cecile Chamenade's "Autumn," and a cello work by Elgar. Both of these were absolutely beautiful and I could not help, nor suppress the tears that welled up in my eyes.

I opened all of the windows of the car and assisted my errant companion to her freedom. She fluttered, stuttered, and then finally left, reminding me of that one moment so long ago in New England. This incident occurred almost exactly ten years from the four-day weekend over which I wrote "Chizuru," in November of 1987.

Donald J. Mangus, M.D.

About the Author

As a plastic and reconstructive surgeon, Don Mangus has traveled to Africa, South Korea, the Philippines, South America, and Mexico, where between 1973 and 1993, he spent a total of a year and a half performing reconstructive surgical procedures. He has traveled overseas independently and with Project Hope, Interplast, Orthopedics Overseas, Care-Medico, and the Medical Benevolent Foundation.

In South Korea, he treated and reconstructed massive burns and their subsequent deformities. In Addis Ababa in Ethiopia when the capital was surrounded by Eritrean rebels, he operated on the mutilating war injuries at the Army Hospital and at the Black Lion Hospital.

Dr. Mangus has great compassion for the victims of war, trauma and disease. As past founder and director of a Northern California burn center, he reflects in this book his great feelings for the victims of the sometimes violent and tragic side of the human experience.

www.ingramcontent.com/pod-product-compliance
Lightning Source LLC
Chambersburg PA
CBHW060749180626
46818CB00002B/514